THE ISLAND STALLION'S FURY

By *Walter Farley*

ILLUSTRATED BY HAROLD ELDRIDGE

RANDOM HOUSE   NEW YORK

2654

FOR A MOST WONDERFUL PERSON
AND MOTHER, MARY E. LUTZ

Contents

THE ISLAND STALLION'S FURY

1

Blue Valley

AZUL ISLAND broke the turquoise blue waters with a startling suddenness. One saw it not as an island but as a massive, egg-shaped boulder dropped into the sea. The islands of the Caribbean Sea are tropical and luxurious in their soft green vegetation and colorful flowers. There was nothing soft or green or colorful about Azul Island.

Its precipitous walls rose naked from the sea, rising a thousand or more feet in the sky until they rounded off to form the dome-shaped top of Azul Island. It was barren and foreboding, with the sea beating white against its barrier walls, seeking entrance and finding none.

Only on large-scale navigation maps of the far eastern area of the Caribbean Sea could the island be found. It ran north and south, nine miles long. But no ships ever passed it unless driven far off their course. Neither did any air lane come within five hundred miles of it. So except for the people of the nearest inhabited island, Antago, a little more than twenty

3

miles to the southwest, Azul Island was little known and untouched.

Only at the southern tip of the island did the mountainous rock break away abruptly to become a low, sandy spit of land where the waves were permitted to roll high upon the shore. This spit was the only part of Azul Island that the people of Antago knew, and very seldom did they have any occasion to visit it.

When they did, they would dock their boats at the narrow wooden pier which was the island's sole connecting link with the outside world, and set out across the dunes of the windswept reef. They would walk up the spit to a small canyon at the end of which was a sheer wall rising five hundred feet above them. They would stop and look up, knowing this was as far as they could go on Azul Island.

"Solid rock," they usually said. "The rest of the island is nothing but rock, eight solid miles of it."

And soon they would leave this desolate, foreboding place, sometimes looking back, once they were at sea, at the bare, yellow rock and the dome-shaped top of Azul Island which gleamed in the sun's rays.

Never, even by the widest stretch of the imagination, could they suspect that running down the dome was a long, narrow gap which allowed the rays of the sun to find a valley . . . a lost valley within a lost world; a valley as soft and green and colorful as any tropical island in the Caribbean Sea. *And it was inhabited!*

Long and narrow, the valley extended almost the length of the island; a bluish-green gem set deep amidst towering walls that were the yellow of pure gold. High up on the wall at the southern end of the valley an underground stream rushed from blackness to sunlight, plummeting downward in a silken sheet of white and crashing onto the rocks of a large pool two hundred feet or more below.

From the great opening where the falls began a trail led down the wall. Halfway to the valley floor it leveled off at a wide ledge fronting a cave. A man sat there, writing. He used empty wooden boxes for his seat and desk, and his pen moved quickly over the paper before him. As he finished each page, he dropped it beside him, and with no hesitation went on to the next sheet.

He was a small man, thin but wiry of build. His knobby knees were uncovered, for he wore tropical walking shorts. Earlier in the day he had put on his white pith helmet to shade his eyes from the glare of the hot sun. He was still wearing the helmet, even though the sun had dropped behind the high walls of the valley. But he hadn't noticed, for he was much too absorbed in his writing. His round tanned face, usually boyish and jovial, was drawn taut from the intensity of his concentration.

He continued writing until two short whistles broke the stillness of the valley. Looking up, he noticed for the first time that it was sunset. The shadows from the walls had reached the valley floor, turning the cropped grass to an almost brilliant blue. His gaze traveled far up the valley where a band of horses was grazing. He tried without success to locate his friend Steve.

The two short whistles came again. Reaching for his high-powered binoculars, the man brought them close to the steel-rimmed glasses he wore. Near the edge of the tall sugar cane which grew wild on the sides of the valley, he located the boy. Apparently Steve had been sitting there watching the mares and foals since his arrival in Blue Valley a few hours ago. But now he was getting to his feet. The man saw him place his fingers to his lips; again came the two short whistles. Steve was calling Flame, but the stallion was nowhere in sight.

Then from far up the valley came an answering scream. Steve's whistles were the softest of whispers compared to it. Shrill, loud and clear, it rose to such a high pitch that it seemed it would shatter the towering walls. And when it finally died the valley echoed to the fast, rhythmic beat of pounding hoofs.

The man moved his binoculars to pick up the running stallion. He was coming through the tall cane far up on the opposite side of the valley, the stalks bending and breaking beneath his giant body. When he reached the short, cropped grass, his strides lengthened as he swept toward the boy who awaited him. He was beautiful, swift and strong, and his chestnut coat and mane were the glowing red of fire.

The man put down his binoculars when the stallion came to a stop before the boy. It's so good to have Steve back again in Blue Valley, he thought. Flame's glad. I'm glad. Everybody's happy. Smiling contentedly, the man turned once more to his writing.

Tall and long limbed, the red stallion stood as motionless as a statue; his small head was raised high, not in defiance but in haughty grandeur. Yet his large eyes never left the boy and there was soft recognition in them. Finally he tossed his head and his heavy mane rose and fell with the high arch of his neck.

"*Flame.*"

Small ears pricked forward at the sound of Steve Duncan's voice. Long, delicate nostrils quivered. Then, without further hesitation, the stallion moved toward the boy.

Steve touched the silken neck and ran his fingers through the tousled mane, gently smoothing it. Flame stood quietly, with only his eyes moving as they turned from Steve to the band that had strayed in the direction of the water pool, then back to the boy again. And knowing now that Flame had not forgotten him during the ten months he had been away,

Steve was content just to stand there beside him and to look at him.

Never was there a horse so beautiful! No other could match the finely molded body or the giant muscles that moved so smoothly beneath tight, sliding skin. No equal did he have in strength of legs and withers, chest and shoulders. And his head was the most beautiful part of him, for every inch of it disclosed the preponderance of Arabian blood that was in this stallion. It was raised high, yet set at an angle, accentuating the high curve at the crest of his long neck. It was wedge-shaped, broad in the forehead and tapering down to long, delicate nostrils. The ears were small and close together; just now they were pricked, almost touching at the tips. The large eyes, set wide apart, were most expressive, glaring wildly when the stallion's fury was aroused and becoming soft and warm when there was nothing to fear or fight.

That Flame had fought often and hard was easily seen in the scars that marked his red coat. Some were jagged, made by the cutting, ravaging teeth of fighting stallions. Others were clean and straight, left by pounding, battering hoofs. Some were old, some new. All of them made this giant stallion what he was, King of the Band. He had won his leadership through fighting; he would lose it the same way.

Steve swept his hands across the muscled withers.

He leaned a little on the stallion's back, and the red coat beneath his hands quivered.

"Oh, Flame," he said. "It's good . . . so good to be back."

For a moment the boy just stood there. Never had this great stallion known the touch of hands before his, he knew. Never had Flame even seen human beings before Steve and his friend Pitch had found Blue Valley late last summer. It had taken time to convince Flame that he and his band had nothing to fear from Steve's and Pitch's presence, nothing to fight. But finally Steve had won the stallion's love and confidence. He'd been able to play with him, run with him, ride him any time of day or night. And now after so many long months he was back with his horse, to continue this life which was as new to him as it was to Flame.

He placed more of his weight on the stallion's back. Flame tossed his head as though he knew what was coming and was impatient to get along with it. Steve leaped as high as he could and pulled himself, face downward, across the stallion's back. Flame whirled while the boy was still hanging on precariously, but Steve's hand found the thick mane and quickly he pulled himself upright as Flame again came to a stop.

The boy pressed his knees close to the withers and then he touched the stallion low on the neck. With short, springy steps Flame lightly crabstepped down the valley. He snorted repeatedly, and his ears shifted, half turning to Steve. He wanted to move out of the crabstep, yet he awaited the boy's command.

Finally Steve moved his leg slightly, his heel rubbing against the stallion. Flame shifted smoothly into a slow, rocking canter. Then his strides lengthened as Steve bent closer to his arched neck. The rhythmic beat of the stallion's hoofs came faster; he tossed his head and occasionally struck out a foreleg either in play or as an indication that he wanted to run all out. Yet he waited for a further command from Steve, and finally the boy hunched his shoulders far forward

and pressed his cheek hard against Flame's silken neck.

Steve felt the ground give way beneath the ever lengthening strides, and the wind whistled until it shut out the pounding hoofs. His eyes filled with the rush of wind and he sought protection from it by burying his head in the stallion's whipping mane.

He had ridden all his life, but this was not riding. This was being part of a horse!

Through blurred eyes he saw that they had almost reached the pool beneath the waterfall. The band moved quickly away, scattering at sight of their

running leader. Steve touched Flame and the stallion swerved obediently away from the pool, cutting across the valley floor to the far side. Steve began talking to him then, and shifted his weight back off the withers. The stallion slowed down, although he pawed repeatedly with his foreleg, striking out in play.

Steve brought him to a stop, and except for tossing his head Flame stood still. The yellow walls had been the only spectators to the exhibition of Flame's blazing speed.

Steve turned his attention to the band. The horses were grazing again. The boy counted over a hundred of them, including all the suckling foals who stayed close beside their dams. And there were weanlings who frolicked and played, glorying in their newly acquired independence from their mothers and testing their strength and speed against one another. Yearlings and older colts and fillies kept to themselves, content in their maturity.

Flame was their leader. They looked to him for protection against any danger and for guidance. Yet Steve knew that some day one of the older colts, falsely secure in his strength and youth, would attempt to take Flame's leadership away from him. They would meet in physical combat, and to live and maintain his supremacy of the band Flame would kill. There could be but one leader of the band. It had been that way for centuries, ever since the Spanish Conquistadores had forsaken the ancestors of these horses in Blue Valley. Forebears who had been left here to die. But who had not died. Instead, they had lived and bred and the band had survived. The horses the Spaniards had forsaken in this valley were of the purest blood and the finest obtainable; they had passed on their speed, stamina and beauty to their offspring. And Blue Valley with its good grass and water and protective walls had fostered these horses until today there was no finer band in all the world.

Steve touched Flame on the neck, stroking him gently. No one knows what Pitch and I have found, he mused. Not even Mother and Dad know or suspect anything out of the ordinary. They like Pitch; he's an old friend of the family. They were glad I wanted to visit him on Antago last year, glad that I wanted to come back again this summer. Mother especially. For when Dad had proposed the long automobile trip for their vacation this summer, she had said, "You and I can do that, Paul. Let Steve visit Pitch again. Let him travel outside the country while he can; there'll be time enough for him to take automobile trips with us."

Steve smiled to himself as he thought of his mother's words. What Mom really had meant was that she was glad he'd be with Pitch. She had great respect for Pitch's intelligence and she thought it would do Steve good to be with him. She thought of Pitch as a scholar, an historian. She knew of his interest in archaeology and that he and Steve were doing some digging on an uninhabited island twenty miles northeast of Antago. Yes, that was what had brought them to the spit of Azul Island. And they had found more than they'd bargained for, much more than they'd ever dreamed of finding. But no one else knew.

Flame moved uneasily beneath him. The stallion wanted to be off with his band, and Steve noticed that it was becoming dark fast. He'd better be getting back to Pitch. He had a lot of questions he wanted to ask him. Touching Flame, he cantered across the valley to the trail which went up to the ledge; there he dismounted and, giving the stallion a light slap on his haunches, watched while Flame returned to his band.

He started up the trail, thinking of all the wonderful days to come, over two months, which he'd be able to spend with Flame and the band in their lost world.

2

Pitch's Map

THE climb to the ledge was steep but not hard, and within a few minutes Steve had reached the campsite. But Phil Pitcher didn't look up from his writing.

"You'll go blind trying to work in the dark, Pitch."

The man raised his head in a quick, startled way. "Oh, it's you, Steve," he said, putting down his pen.

"Not expecting anyone else, were you?" Steve asked, smiling.

"No. No, of course not. It was just that I was so absorbed." Pitch paused to remove his glasses and rub his eyes, then he too smiled. "You're right. It *is* almost dark. I'll just put these papers away."

Steve turned on the Coleman gasoline lantern, and his eyes blinked in its bright yellow light. He watched Pitch pick up the pages of the work he had done that day and place them carefully in his leather briefcase before putting it just within the cave's entrance. At the base of the opposite wall were three shovels, two picks, an axe and a pile of rope. Beside them were two rolled sleeping bags and a half-filled box of canned foods. In the center of the ledge was a small but efficient two-plate kerosene stove, and next to it all the pots, pans and eating utensils they'd ever need. Just within the entrance of the cave Steve saw a box containing two flashlights, a camera, more tools and a pile of other things. Yes, during the ten months he'd been away from Blue Valley, Pitch had well equipped the camp with supplies from Antago.

"You're writing about everything?" he asked Pitch, who was buckling the straps of his briefcase.

"Yes, Steve. I began with our finding the entrance to the tunnels, and then have gone on covering just about everything I've seen and done during the time you've been away. I've given a detailed account of every discovery, every trip I've taken through the tunnels. I've taken photographs of Blue Valley, the smaller valley and the canyons and gorges. Also, I've given what I believe from my findings is an accurate history of the island. I've stated that I believe that this island, like Cuba and Puerto Rico, was used as a supply base by the Spaniards during their conquest of the New World. From here they equipped their armies with provisions and weapons . . ."

"And horses," Steve interrupted.

"Yes, horses," Pitch agreed. "Horses of purest blood, they were. The very finest specimens of their race to be obtained in Spain. Horses who faced the battles and world-shaking adventures with the men of Cortés, the Pizarros and DeSoto in their conquest of the Americas!" Pitch's eyes were bright with his enthusiasm. "I've mentioned, too, Steve, that I believe this island was the Spaniards' very last stronghold in the Caribbean Sea. I feel that when the English and French drove back the Spanish armies in the latter part of the seventeenth century, the Spaniards retreated to this natural fortress. But in time they had to forsake this island hurriedly, and they left behind the ancestors of the horses we have in Blue Valley today."

Pitch walked over to the stove, and Steve followed. "But you're not finished with your work, are you, Pitch?" he asked quickly.

"Oh, no, not by any means, Steve. There's much more I want to add to it, many more years of excavation work, tunnel explorations and writing before the complete job is done the way I want to do it and I can send my manuscript to an historical society."

The boy's tense body relaxed as he listened to his friend. He knew that when Pitch finished his work and his discoveries were made public this world would no longer belong solely to them. But Pitch had said that it would take years before his work was complete. The longer it took the better, Steve felt. He loved Flame and his band and Blue Valley too much just as they were to be ashamed of feeling as he did.

Pitch was speaking again. "Oh, and I've drawn a map of the island," he said. "It's not a very professional map, but I want to show it to you."

He went to the wooden box just within the cave's entrance and withdrew a large, rolled paper. He placed it on the box he'd used for a table, then called Steve while unrolling the map.

"Now," he said, looking up at the night sky, "let's pretend we're up there over Azul Island and looking down. Not that you'd actually be able to see much of what I have on this map if you were in a plane flying over Azul Island," he explained hurriedly. "If that ever did happen—and it never has so far—and you could get close enough to the dome, you'd know there was a valley down here, but little more. Anyway," he continued, "it's just the effect I want you to have. Try to put yourself up there and pretend you've got x-ray eyes so you can see right through the rock to the tunnels when necessary." He laughed at his last remark, then took a pencil from his pocket and placed the point on the map.

"Here's the island, running north and south. We'll start at the southern end, the spit of land and the pier. Last summer you and I walked up the spit to the canyon at the end. I call it Spit Canyon on the map. We stopped at the end and looked up at the wall. About

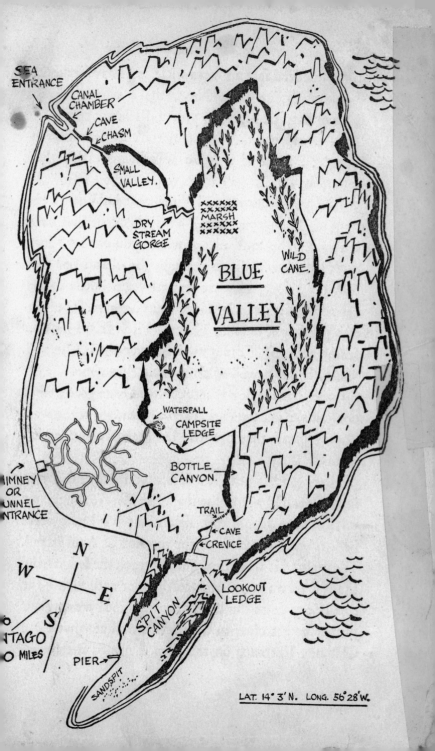

SEA
ENTRANCE

CANAL
CHAMBER

CAVE
CHASM

SMALL
VALLEY

DRY
STREAM
GORGE

MARSH

WILD
CANE

BLUE

VALLEY

WATERFALL
CAMPSITE
LEDGE

BOTTLE
CANYON

CHIMNEY
OR
TUNNEL
ENTRANCE

TRAIL

CAVE
CREVICE

LOOKOUT
LEDGE

N

W

E

S

O
NTAGO
O MILES

SPIT
CANYON

PIER

SANDSPIT

LAT. 14° 3′ N. LONG. 56° 28′ W.

three hundred feet up we saw a ledge. I have it marked Lookout Ledge here. Now, that's where we saw Flame that first night, so you and I knew the rest of Azul Island couldn't be solid rock as everyone believed . . . not if a horse was living inside there somewhere.

"Do you follow me?" Pitch asked. When Steve nodded, Pitch continued. "Well, back of that ledge is a cave and narrow chasm which you can't see from the spit below. We go through the chasm and then down a steep trail that leads to the bottle-shaped canyon . . . I call it Bottle Canyon here. The canyon goes right to Blue Valley." Pitch raised his eyes from the map. "Comes in right over there," he said.

On the same wall as their camp, but almost at the far side of the valley where the wild cane grew, Steve could make out the dark, narrow cleavage in the wall. "I've noticed that canyon, but never went up it," he said.

"Let's get back to the spit again," Pitch said, bringing his pencil back to the map. "When we saw Flame on Lookout Ledge that first night we knew there had to be an entrance to the interior of Azul Island. We realized it wasn't possible to reach the ledge from the spit so we went back to the pier and, taking the small dory from the launch, rowed until we saw our chance to get close to the barrier wall at what I call Chimney Entrance on this map. I named it that because we climbed the cleft in the wall and went down the ventilation shaft we found on top, which is much like a chimney.

"And that took us into the tunnels," he added quietly.

Pitch paused and Steve did not urge him to go on. Each remembered that only by the grace of God had they found their way out of the tunnels and were alive to discuss them now.

Finally Pitch moved his pencil over the multitude of lines he had drawn on the map to indicate the tunnels. "This is not a true picture of the direction or number of tunnels," he said. "On this map I'm just giving you an idea of where they are. The work of plotting them accurately is a big job and one I'm not yet prepared to tackle."

"But you do know them, Pitch."

"Only some of them, Steve; a small percentage of the great number that make up this maze. They're a world of their own . . . an underground world.

"But to go back to this map," he went on. "From the tunnels we come to Blue Valley at the top of the waterfall. Then here's the trail leading down the wall to our present campsite overlooking the valley. Now, you know the rest of this pretty well, the way we get to our launch. But I want to go over it anyway. About two miles up the valley we find the marsh, right here."

Pitch's pencil found the crossed marks on the left side of the valley which designated the marsh; then simultaneously he and Steve looked up in the direction of the valley. But it was too dark for them to see anything of the marsh. They turned back to the map.

"Here on the other side of the marsh," Pitch continued, "is the dry gorge of the stream that once emptied into the marsh. We follow it until we come to the little valley. I just call it Small Valley on the map," he explained. "Crossing that valley, we enter the chasm and cave which take us to the sea entrance. And there, as you know, we have our launch in the great chamber, making it possible for us to come and go as we please . . . using the very same entrance the Conquistadores used in bringing their armies and supplies into this stronghold."

Pitch began rolling the map. "Well, that's it, Steve."

"It's a good job. As good a job as any professional could have done."

"No," said Pitch with a smile. "But it's the best I can do, and I'm glad it's clear to you." Putting away the map, he urged, "Let's eat now, Steve. I've spent too much time talking, and you must be hungry and tired. It's been a hard day for you."

Early the next morning after breakfast, Pitch took his light pick and placed his flashlights in the small leather bag which he carried over his shoulder.

"You're sure I can't help you?" Steve asked.

"No. I've found an interesting tunnel. I can travel it better alone."

"You're careful?"

"Very careful, Steve. I won't get lost. I mark every tunnel I travel. I'll show you later today, if you'd like to go inside with me."

"I would," Steve replied.

"I'll be back by noon." As Pitch started up the trail, he said over his shoulder, "I'm taking it for granted you want to spend this morning with Flame and the others."

After Pitch had disappeared within the great opening at the top of the waterfall, Steve looked about for Flame. The giant stallion had left his band several times during the last hour to come down the valley, his head raised in the direction of the ledge, looking for the boy. But Flame was back with the band now, grazing with them.

Steve went down the trail and started up the valley floor. He hadn't gone very far when Flame saw him. Lifting his head, the stallion neighed, then went back to his grazing. But only for a moment. He stopped, then trotted toward the boy.

Steve watched his horse, felt the muscles of his throat tighten at the beauty and grace of this spirited stallion. And he marveled and was humble that Flame belonged to him. During the months that he had been away from Blue Valley, he had often thought that it all had been a dream, that there was no such place as Azul Island, no such horse as Flame, no lost band living in a lost world.

When Flame stopped before him, Steve touched the soft nose of the stallion, ran his hand between the large, bright eyes and then down the soft neck. He stood stroking his horse for a long time, straightening the red mane and forelock which hung low over Flame's forehead.

Finally he mounted and, letting the stallion choose his gait, rode toward the band. The mares with suckling foals at their sides moved away at sight of him, but the long-legged weanlings stood their ground, inquisitively watching his approach. They scattered when Flame neighed shrilly, and Steve laughed as they pushed hard against each other in their wild efforts to get out of the path of their running leader.

Flame moved past the band, his strides lengthening. Letting him go, Steve rode low and close to the stallion's neck. For all of a mile Flame went at a full gallop, then Steve spoke to him and sat back. The stallion responded, slowing down to a canter and then a trot.

They were on the left side of the valley, near the marsh. Already gray vapors were beginning to rise from the swampland in the heat of the sun's first rays. The hollow which fostered the marsh was no more than a hundred yards deep and ran for perhaps a quarter of a mile along this side of the valley. But to reach the dry-stream gorge which cut the barrier wall here one had to pass through the marsh. Luckily there were green avenues of solid ground that made it possible to avoid the quagmires.

Steve turned Flame away from the desolate marsh and back toward the band. This morning he wanted to go through the canyon which led to the ledge overlooking the spit of land. Bottle Canyon, he reminded himself—that's what Pitch calls it on his map. I'd better call it that, too. And the ledge overlooking the spit is Lookout Ledge. I guess Pitch named it that because from that ledge the Spaniards could have seen any approach from Antago and the south.

He gave Flame his head, and the stallion went into his long, effortless lope down the valley. A group of yearling colts and fillies broke and ran at Flame's approach. Steve watched them go, then turned to look at the mares and foals grazing near the wild cane. Next to Flame he loved the foals best. It was fun watching them as they stayed so close to their mothers, seeking protection from anything that might frighten or startle them.

But soon the band was left far behind and they had reached the water pool. Flame stretched down to drink. When he had finished Steve took him along the southern wall of the valley toward the wild cane on the opposite side. Just before they reached it, they came to the cleavage in the wall. Steve turned Flame into the long neck of Bottle Canyon.

The ground was soft with good grass and free of rock. Flame went from a walk to a trot, and Steve let him go. For a hundred yards the high walls of the canyon rose close on either side, then they widened, forming the great base of Bottle Canyon.

The grass here too was good and cropped low, so Steve knew that Flame used the canyon for grazing. The high yellow walls rose all around them and Steve didn't see where it was possible to reach Lookout Ledge from the canyon floor. But Flame seemed to know where he was going, so Steve let him alone.

The stallion went toward the far wall, which Steve knew was the only barrier between them and the spit. As they neared it, Flame veered to the right, and Steve saw the trail running up along the right wall. He thought it too steep and narrow, and sought to check Flame's speed. But the stallion only shook his head, then gathered himself and lurched up the trail. The first few feet were the steepest part of the climb; from there on the ascent was much more gradual than it had appeared from below. Steve noticed the regular cuttings in the rock on either side of the trail; the Spaniards must have widened this path to Lookout Ledge.

Halfway up the wall, Flame entered a high natural cleft in the stone. The light grew dim but the sky could be seen overhead. Farther on the chasm narrowed until Steve could touch the walls on either side of Flame. He looked up. There was no opening overhead. Quickly he checked Flame's walk. Then he saw that the light ahead was as bright as day. Also, the walls had widened. They were in a large shallow cave that opened on Lookout Ledge!

Steve brought Flame to a stop and slid off his back. He moved cautiously toward the ledge, looking back once to make certain that Flame was not following him. There was only one chance in a thousand that anyone from Antago would be visiting the spit of Azul Island, but he mustn't take even that one chance of being seen.

Lookout Ledge was a good deal larger than it appeared from below. It was about fifty feet long and thirty feet wide. Flat on his stomach, Steve crawled across the ledge until he was able to look down three hundred feet below to the floor of Spit Canyon. Beyond was the sandy, windswept land and the sea. There was no human being in the canyon or on the spit, no boat at sea.

But grazing on the tufts of grass in the canyon was the small band of horses that lived on the spit. There were eight mares with foals by their sides and a stallion—all small, wiry and shaggy. These were the horses that had brought him to Azul Island last year, for Pitch had written him about this band.

They were supposed to be descendants of the horses the Conquistadores rode during the Conquest, according to the story which the Chamber of Commerce on Antago released to newspapers in the United States and South America every few years in one form or another. But no one knew whether the story was true. Steve and Pitch, having found Flame and his band in Blue Valley, knew that the story could be closer to the truth than most people on Antago actually believed. On Antago, the "wise" citizens said that the story was just one that had been promoted by the publicity-minded Chamber of Commerce to get the name of Antago in foreign newspapers and possibly build up the island's tourist trade. These people claimed that actually the horses were from Antago—that many years ago they had been taken to the spit of Azul Island and released to propagate and create the basis for such an interesting and romantic story!

Steve didn't know the correct answer any more than anyone else did, although he and Pitch had discussed the small band very often. The horses had none of the characteristics of Flame and his band. But then, as Pitch had said, the ancestors of these horses may have been those which hadn't met the high

equine standards of the Conquistadores, so the Spaniards had kept them on the spit and away from their
favorites which grazed in Blue Valley. Then, too, the
spit being what it was, windswept and with scarcely
any grass, it was only natural that the horses would be
very much unlike those of Blue Valley in size and
quality.

Steve heard Flame behind him. He got to his feet
to stand beside the stallion. Flame's ears were pitched
forward, his nostrils dilated. He neighed to the mares
below. The band scattered, the mares whinnying.
Only the small stallion stood his ground. He raised
his head, whistling. Flame's answering challenge shattered the cry of the rival stallion. Then Flame moved
uneasily up and down the ledge, his red body trembling in his eagerness to fight.

Steve went back to the cave, calling Flame and
hoping he'd follow him. He kept walking and calling,
but only when he was nearing the trail did he hear
Flame's hoofbeats behind him. He began his descent
to the floor of Bottle Canyon with the stallion following him.

Later, when they walked into Blue Valley, Steve
looked toward camp and saw that Pitch had already
returned. Flame moved away from Steve, cantering
toward his band. The boy watched him until he heard
the sudden breaking of the cane stalks on his right.
Turning around, he saw a heavy bay mare making her

way alone through the tall cane. He watched her until she came to a stop in a small clearing not far from the wall. From her size and actions he knew she'd be giving birth to a foal sometime during the afternoon or night.

Steve turned away. He was going to take a special interest in this foal to come, for never had he seen a newly born foal. He'd watch the mare carefully and, if possible, go to her the moment the foal was born. Would it be a colt or filly? Would it be a red chestnut like Flame or a dark brown bay like the mare?

Feeling like the luckiest and happiest boy in the world, he shouted to Pitch and burst into a run to tell him about the foal to come.

3

The Bay Mare

FINISH your beans, Steve," Pitch said a little sternly, "and stop watching that bay mare. She won't have her foal during the daytime. Mares are just like women; they have their babies at the most unreasonable hours of the night . . . just to make it hard on you," he added, smiling.

Steve smiled too. "How do you know, Pitch? You're a bachelor." Finished with his beans, he put the empty plate in a pail of hot water.

"What was the name of that couple who ran the boarding house on your block?" Pitch asked in reply to Steve's question.

"Mr. and Mrs. Reynolds," the boy answered. "You ought to remember . . . you lived there five years."

Nodding, Pitch said, "Yep. And she had three children while I was there. They all were born between three and five o'clock in the morning. Mr. Reynolds and I often discussed how unreasonable it was of Mrs. Reynolds."

"But children and foals *can* be born during the day-time," Steve insisted.

"Perhaps, but I doubt it."

Steve reached for the can of powdered milk and, removing the lid, put several tablespoonfuls of the powder into a pint jar half-filled with water. He stirred briskly until the powder was thoroughly mixed with the water, then raised the jar to his lips and drank.

"This powdered milk is just like the real thing," he told Pitch, when he had finished.

"It *is* the real thing. It's whole milk. All you did was add water."

Steve glanced again at the clearing on the far side of the valley. The bay mare was standing up, grazing. She seemed to be in no hurry to have her foal. Perhaps Pitch was right and she wouldn't have her foal for hours and hours. He washed the dishes while Pitch fingered the cat-o'-nine-tails he had found in the tunnels that morning.

When Steve had finished, he took the short-handled whip which Pitch offered him for examination. He felt the nine knotted leather lines, each about three feet long, which were fastened to the handle.

"The Spaniards used it for flogging?" he asked Pitch.

"I guess so . . . sometimes," the man replied quietly.

"Then in many ways Tom is like them," Steve said. "Tom and his bull whip."

Pitch went over to the stove to clean it. It was obvious that he didn't want to discuss the stepbrother with whom he'd lived on Antago for the last three years.

"Flame and I went to Lookout Ledge today," Steve said after a while. "We saw the band there— eight mares with foals, and the stallion. Tom must have taken all the weanlings and yearlings in his round-up last year."

"I guess so," Pitch said, moving away.

Steve's eyes wore an expression of concern as they followed Pitch. No matter how often he'd tried he couldn't get Pitch to talk about Tom. Tom had been commissioned by the government of Antago to re-move the surplus horses from the spit of Azul Island every five years. He would leave a small band to propagate . . . at the present time it consisted of the eight mares and a stallion. Tom sold the horses for what he could get and took his fee, the remainder of the money going to the government of Antago. But the meager sum of money received for the small, wiry horses wasn't important either to Tom or the government. Steve knew that Tom acted as agent solely for the pleasure of gathering and then breaking these horses to his iron hand and will. The govern-ment was interested in Tom's "wild horse round-up" solely because of the pictures and stories they could place in foreign newspapers as a result of it. It was one of these pictures that Pitch had sent him last summer.

Tom hadn't been at his Antago sugar cane plantation when Steve had arrived from the United States a few days ago. And all Pitch had told him was that Tom was away. Nothing more, even though he'd asked several times.

Steve didn't want to think about Tom any more than Pitch did, so he turned his thoughts now on Flame. The stallion had taken his band far up the valley and Steve was thinking of joining them when Pitch called to him from the entrance of the cave.

"I want to show you some of the things I've found in the tunnels and chambers," Pitch said, taking the lantern. "I have them in here."

They walked to the far end of the cave, and Pitch placed the lighted lantern beside a wooden box. Removing the lid, he began taking out the relics that were there. With great care, he placed them on the ground one at a time . . . a tarnished silver goblet, a horseshoe, a heavy shoe stirrup of solid bronze, beautifully engraved; a short sword, a long lance or spear, which the Conquistadores carried into battle; a helmet and a coat of mail with its interlinked rings and riveted ends to protect the wearer; and more, much more. It took Pitch all of fifteen minutes to remove his precious relics from the box and show them to Steve.

"I don't believe there's a finer private collection in all the world," Pitch said proudly as he put the things back in the box.

When they left the cave, they stood for a while on the ledge overlooking Blue Valley. Flame and his band were far away. The bay mare was still grazing in the clearing.

"Want to see a little of the tunnels this afternoon, Steve?" Pitch asked. "I'd especially like to show you where I have all our extra supplies stored."

He led the way up the trail to the waterfall, then stopped at the great opening where the underground stream flowed. Taking a flashlight from his shoulder bag, he said, "I want you to enter these tunnels only in case of an emergency. And always take this bag, Steve. There are three flashlights in it, extra batteries and bulbs. Being without light in the tunnels is certain death. Come now."

Steve followed him along the underground stream; the light grew dim and the drone of the falls lessened. As they made their way around a wide, gradual curve, Steve saw only blackness ahead. Pitch clicked on the flashlight; his pace never slackened as he followed its beam.

They must have walked for more than fifteen minutes when Pitch came to a sudden stop and flashed the light on the wall beside him. Steve could see letters and figures marked in chalk on the wall. A few feet away there was another tunnel.

"We turn right here," Pitch said. "All these letters and figures mean something to me. They're a code I use so I'll always know where I am. I've placed them at every fork, every turn in the tunnels. But for our purpose now, and for your use later if you ever need to get additional provisions and I'm not around, I want you to look only for the letter C and to follow any tunnels in which you find a C marked with the other letters. That's all you need to know."

He turned into the tunnel, flashed his light on the wall to show Steve the letter C that was included with other letters and numerals, then kept on going.

Soon they came to a fork from which three tunnels extended. Pitch flashed his light on the walls. Only the tunnel on the extreme left included the letter C. Now they walked hunched over, for the ceiling was low.

Steve stayed close to Pitch, marveling at his friend's knowledge of this underground world and hoping that never would he have to travel the tunnels alone. He knew from what Pitch had told him that some great disturbance of Nature in an early archaeological age had created these tunnels . . . that much was evident from their great number and the jagged, shattered ceilings. But the smoothness of some of the floors, the perfect regularity of the cutting on each side were the work of Man . . . so many hundreds of men, slaves of the Conquistadores, for so many years!

The ceiling of the tunnel was higher now and they were able to stand upright. Suddenly Pitch stopped, and Steve saw the high opening of a great chamber on his left. He knew where he was then. He had been in this chamber before.

There was a dim, gray light within and Steve remembered the ventilation shaft that penetrated the ceiling of this room. Pitch was standing beneath it, looking up, and Steve joined him. Through the box-like shaft they could see the blue sky hundreds of feet above them. The air coming down was fresh and cool.

Pitch directed the beam of his flashlight to a far corner of the chamber and there Steve saw several boxes of canned goods, more shovels, picks, lanterns and flashlights.

"But why keep all these extra supplies and equipment in here and not back at camp?" Steve asked.

"Just as an emergency measure," Pitch replied.

"I don't get it, Pitch. There's no reason why this stuff wouldn't be as safe back at camp as here."

The man laughed. "You're probably right, Steve. But I've always been one for keeping my valuables in two places, so I won't lose everything at one time. I guess that's the reason I keep half my money in my pocket and the rest in my wallet. That's just in case somebody should steal my wallet." He laughed again. "But no one ever has."

"I guess you're right," Steve said.

"Anyway," Pitch went on, "sometimes when I'm working in the tunnels it's easier for me to come here than go to camp. I even have a small stove here, Steve."

Pitch flashed the light on a long wooden table and chair which had been there when he and Steve had found the chamber the previous year. "I do some writing here occasionally, too. And just think—I use the very same table and chair the Conquistadores' leaders used!"

He flashed the light on the wall behind the table and there, inscribed in the stone, was a coat of arms— a large shield with a lion at the top holding a bird clutched between his paws. Below was the date, 1669.

They stayed there for a few minutes longer, then returned to Blue Valley.

During the late afternoon, the bay mare left the clearing once to get a drink of water. Then she went back, carefully stepping along as though not to jostle the foal she was carrying. Night fell and Steve knew that he'd have to wait until morning to find out whether the mare had had her foal.

Lying on his blanket, Steve listened to the steady

drone of the waterfall, hoping that it would bring him sleep. But it didn't help. Pitch was turning restlessly in his sleep. Steve wondered if it was his friend's uneasiness that was keeping him so wide awake. Or was it just his thinking about the bay mare? But that's silly, he told himself; she can have her foal without any help from me. And morning will be time enough for me to find out what's happened. No, it can't be the mare that's keeping me awake. Maybe I'm just not tired. But I should be. It's been a long day . . . a good day.

Closing his eyes, he tried to fall asleep. The nickering of the mares came to him and occasionally he heard Flame's sharp, piercing call as the stallion moved with his band.

There were so many good days to look forward to, Steve thought . . . the rest of June, all of July and August, and part of September before he'd have to leave again. Over two months to be spent with Flame and the band. Nothing in the world could be more wonderful than the days to come!

But again he opened his eyes, wide awake. *Was he thinking of Tom Pitcher?* Were Pitch's evasive answers to his questions about Tom bothering him more than he let on? Tom was nothing like Pitch. There was no blood relationship, for Pitch's father had adopted Tom as a baby and had given him his name. Pitch and Tom had grown up together in England, then separated, with Tom joining the British army and going to India while Pitch left home to attend school in the United States. After college, Pitch had stayed on in America until two years ago when he heard Tom had a plantation on Antago and decided to join him.

Tom had changed a great deal in the many years he and Pitch had been separated. Tom was hard and ruthless and, at times, cruel. Steve had seen all these things for himself last summer. He had seen too that Pitch was afraid of Tom, just as he was.

But he didn't want to think of Tom Pitcher. There was no reason to think of him here, where Tom could never bother them. Steve closed his eyes and thought only of Flame and the band and the bay mare . . . until finally he fell asleep.

He awakened with the first heavy gray light of early morning. He could just make out the band grazing far up the valley. Pitch was still sleeping. Suddenly Steve remembered the bay mare and his eyes turned quickly to the clearing. He couldn't see her; she was down or had left the clearing. Without awakening Pitch he hurried down the trail.

Reaching the valley floor, he ran until he came to the wild cane, then bent low, cautiously stealing through the stalks. If the mare was having her foal, he didn't want to disturb her. He only wanted to watch and help her if necessary. She could have left the clearing to have her foal in some more secluded spot, but he doubted it; it was more than likely that she was here.

He was close to the clearing when he saw the mare. She had got to her feet and now stood quietly. Her black mane was tousled and matted with long blades of grass. Her brown coat was sweated. She looked over the cane, but did not see the boy. She whinnied and her head went down.

Steve knew she'd had her foal. Quietly he moved closer to the clearing. If she didn't see him she wouldn't know he was there for he was downwind from her and she couldn't pick up his scent. He stopped dead still when the mare uttered a short squeal. After a few minutes he rose cautiously to look over the cane. The mare was still standing quietly, her head extended downward. Steve guessed the foal was nursing and that everything was all right. He ducked below the cane again and sat there for a while. He didn't want to disturb the mare now; the foal needed her milk.

Finally he got to his feet and, seeing that the bay mare was walking about the clearing, rose to his full height. She stopped when she saw him. He stood there without moving and talked to her in a soft, low voice. For a minute she watched him, then turned away, and Steve knew she was not very frightened or upset by his presence.

Again he moved forward, talking all the while. He could not see the foal yet. But just a few yards more and he'd be able to see him . . . or would it be a filly? And would it have Flame's red chestnut coat and mane or would it be a bay like the mare? He could hear its movements now, tiny hoofs shuffling alongside the mare. Another few yards and Steve stood on the edge of the clearing.

He saw the foal, a filly! She was standing close beside the mare and nursing again. Her coat was still wet, and her mane was nothing but a stubble of hair; yet Steve could tell she was going to be chestnut colored, like her sire.

Steve watched them for several minutes before he became conscious of the slight movement to his left. Turning quickly, he saw the other foal. *Twins!* The mare had had twins! He knew the odds against such a thing happening were one in ten thousand. And the odds were even greater, a hundred thousand to one, against twin foals living.

The second foal was struggling to its feet. This one, too, had the red chestnut coloring of Flame. *But it was a colt!* Steve watched him stand unsteadily on teetering long legs, afraid to move lest he lose his balance and fall. With large fuzzy eyes the colt looked at the mare, then very slowly and carefully attempted to turn his head toward Steve. But he lost his balance and fell.

Steve went to him, his arms going around the soft, wet limbs. He picked him up, putting him on his feet again and supporting the wobbling body. He felt much of the unsteadiness leave the colt as he held him. Soft large eyes looked into his own; then the colt nuzzled him and Steve knew he was hungry and looking for food.

"Not me," he said, turning to the mare. "She's the one." He saw that the filly had finished nursing. "You're next," he said, turning back to the colt. But he suspected he might have trouble getting the mare to allow this second foal to nurse. Steve had read that when this rare event of foaling twins happened, the mare was very apt to favor one foal, giving it all of her attention while neglecting the other. Picking up the colt in his arms, he carried him toward the mare, hoping desperately that she would accept him.

The mare moved away at his approach, but she didn't leave the clearing, for the filly was not yet ready to follow her. Turning her head around, she stood still and watched as Steve placed the colt on his feet next to the filly. Two pairs of soft, wondrous eyes looked at each other; then the filly, her first hunger having been satisfied and stronger for the nourishment she'd had, moved her stilted legs alongside the colt, pushing him in her efforts to nuzzle him. He would have fallen again if Steve had not been holding him.

The boy watched the mare, calling to her all the while, coaxing her to come to them. Her anxious eyes were on the foals yet she made no move toward them. Again the colt nuzzled Steve, seeking the milk he needed so desperately if he were to live.

Steve waited no longer for the mare to come to him. Lifting the colt, he carried him slowly toward the mare. She shied and trotted around him, returning to the filly. Steve followed her, moving with her as she circled the clearing. Finally she came to a stop, and Steve succeeded in shoving the colt gently but firmly toward her belly. The mare's ears swept back as the colt touched her. Viciously she reached down and bit him, causing the blood to come; then she whirled and took the filly to the far side of the clearing. Steve bent over and lifted the colt to carry him to the mare again. But when he straightened up he found she was going through the cane with the filly close behind.

Steve stood there holding the little colt. As he watched the mare and filly go up the valley to join the band, he realized that what he held in his arms was an *orphaned* foal!

4

Orphaned Foal

THE foal never moved while Steve held him with one arm around his chest, the other beneath his rump. The eyes of the boy and the colt were the same, dazed and unseeing.

Finally Steve turned his eyes away from the valley and focused them upon the foal.

What was he going to do with him? How could he get him back to the mare? And if he didn't how could he keep him alive?

Bewilderment left his eyes now to be replaced by worry, concern, even fear for the life of this soft, slippery foal in his arms.

Don't get excited, he told himself. Put him down. Put him down. You can't do anything with him in your arms. Be calm. You'll get him back to the mare. Everything will be all right. Pitch will help you. *Pitch!*

He put down the foal and turned quickly in the direction of the ledge. "Pitch!" he shouted. But there was no answer from his friend, no sign of him. Pitch was still sleeping.

Again Steve let his eyes travel over the foal standing so close beside him. The tiny hoofs never moved, but the skinny body with ribs showing prominently beneath the wet coat wavered a little. Steve put a hand on him to steady him.

"You'll be all right," he said in a broken voice. He tried to get a grip on himself, then repeated his words, more convincingly this time. He spoke for his own benefit as much as for the foal's. "She'll come back. I know she'll come back to you."

But he wasn't at all certain of this. And with that knowledge fear rose within him again. If the mare didn't return for her foal, or if he couldn't get him to her, the colt would die.

Why hadn't he left the mare alone? Why couldn't he have stayed away from the clearing? If he had not been there to pick up the colt, to confuse the mare, she might have accepted both her twins. He knew nothing about a foaling mare. It would have been so much better if he had just left her alone!

"But she might have abandoned the colt anyway," Steve said aloud in his own defense. "I know that . . . I read it somewhere . . . or someone told me."

The colt turned large blurred eyes upon him, not understanding what had happened.

Steve fought the fear still rising within him.

You've got to do something, he told himself. Try to remember what you've read in all those horse books. *Try to remember!*

I will. I will, he promised. I'll try to remember. Foaling mares. Newly born foals. There were chapters on it. Twin foals. There was something on twin foals. When a mare has twins, she may very often neglect one foal . . . *Neglect* . . . *not abandon.* Nothing I ever read said the mare completely abandons one of her twins. So she might accept this colt, take him back, if I can only get him to her!

Steve got to his feet and ran from the clearing. With Pitch's help he might be able to do it! But once more in the wild cane he came to a sudden stop and turned back. Gradually he was recalling what he'd read should be done for a newly born foal. He grabbed several large green leaves from the cane stalks on his way back to the clearing.

Dropping to his knees before the foal, Steve cleaned the mucus from the small nostrils so the colt would have no trouble breathing; he removed some from the corners of the eyes which now were slowly, very slowly, following his movements. He ran the dry leaves over the wet coat. Soon the sun would be over the walls of the valley, drying the foal more thoroughly than he could do now.

Getting to his feet, Steve touched the colt on his

short stubble of a mane, then ran from the clearing. But again he stopped after running only a few yards, and looked back.

The foal was watching him, had even taken a few steps toward him.

Steve went back to pick him up, to carry him. The small body was quiet in his arms, the head turned a little toward him, wet nostrils lightly touching him.

Steve tripped on the cane stalks but regained his balance and his grip on the slippery coat. He shifted the foal in his arms; it weighed only about forty or fifty pounds, and most of the weight was in its long, stilted legs. When he reached the cropped grass of the valley, Steve found it easier to carry him.

"Pitch! Pitch!" he shouted. There was movement on the ledge, but no response. "Pitch!"

Steve was almost directly beneath the ledge when Pitch rose to his feet and looked down. Steve shouted to him again.

Pitch flicked his eyes over at the band up the valley, then back to Steve again.

"Put that foal down and let him go back to his dam," he shouted. "She'll be after you, if you don't."

"She left him! Please come down, Pitch. Please!"

"What?"

"His dam doesn't want him. She let him go!" Steve shouted.

Pitch started down the trail.

After lowering the colt to the ground, Steve backed away from him slowly. The stilt-legs moved cautiously a few steps, then stopped. The head turned a little toward Steve, and the foal would have lost his balance and fallen had it not been for the boy's quick hands.

Pitch was now beside him. "What's happened, Steve?" His words were clipped in his excitement. "Where's his dam? He's just been born, hasn't he?"

"She had twins, Pitch. *Twins!*" Steve's voice was high in spite of his efforts to be calm.

"You mean . . . well, where is she? Why isn't she taking care of this one? What's happened to her? Where is she?" Pitch was just as excited as Steve. And perhaps it was this that helped the boy regain a little of his own composure.

"I was there when it happened. She just ran off with the other . . . a filly. We've got to get him to her, Pitch! He needs her."

"Yes, yes, I know that. But where is she?"

"Back with the band."

"Then let's take him to her . . . that's all we have to do."

"But that isn't all, Pitch," Steve said.

"Not all? Why isn't it?"

"She has to accept him."

Pitch didn't say anything right away. His puzzled gaze turned from Steve to the foal at the boy's side.

Then, "Why won't she accept him? She's his mother, isn't she?"

As patiently as he could, Steve explained all that had happened.

When he had finished, Pitch said, his voice rising again, "But she can't do that! This foal needs her. He's got to have her. He'll die!"

Once more Steve lifted the colt and held the trembling body. "We'll take turns carrying him up the valley," he said.

They had just started when Flame came down to meet them. He stopped beside Steve, but didn't touch the foal.

Steve talked to the stallion but kept walking. He realized that Flame sensed something was wrong.

"Careful, Steve," Pitch warned. "He might think you're going to hurt this foal. Let me take the colt; you handle Flame. It'll be better all round."

Steve gave the foal to Pitch, then turned to Flame, putting a hand on his arched neck. The stallion was tense, excited. He kept watching the foal, never taking his eyes off him. Steve stayed close to him, careful but not afraid.

After a short while he took the foal again, talking to Flame all the time. "We're not hurting him," he said. "We're taking him back." The foal raised his head a little when Flame bent down and sniffed him. Their noses had only touched when the stallion drew back quickly. Bolting, he moved ahead of them, whirled and came back. As he walked beside them again, Steve noticed that much of the stallion's restlessness was gone. Perhaps Flame in some way now sensed what had happened. At least, he knew they meant no harm to this foal.

Steve saw the bay mare grazing with the others. Beside her was her filly, nursing again.

Pitch said, glancing at the foal in Steve's arms, "He looks terribly weak. How long can they go without food, Steve?"

"I don't know, Pitch. But he needs some pretty soon. He's so little."

They stopped, for the band was less than a hundred yards away and some of the mares had turned in their direction. The suckling foals moved away first, running behind their mothers for the protection afforded by their large bodies.

"Don't startle them," Steve warned, "or we'll never catch up to them."

"What should we do then?" Pitch asked. "How are we ever going to get close enough to them to do any good?"

Steve moved forward. "A little closer, then we'll put him down," he said. "We can just hope his dam will take him when she sees him alone."

"Maybe she's forgotten by now she ever had him," was Pitch's retort.

Steve was silent.

They left the foal not more than fifty yards from the band, and walked back down the valley. Only when they were a good distance away did they stop and watch to see what would happen to the foal.

Flame had followed them but now he too stopped, midway between them and the foal. He seemed undecided whether to go to Steve or return to the colt, who stood alone, bewildered and waiting.

For a while nothing happened. The foal stood as still as a statue, his eyes fixed on the band. Over the eastern wall of the valley came the sun, its rays finding him and drying his wet coat; his eyes blinked in this new light. But he remained still, never moving.

"The band means nothing to him without his mother to guide him," Pitch said in a low voice. "He doesn't even know they're his kind. He doesn't belong."

The bay mare moved away from the band, the filly staying close by her side. "Watch her," Steve said hopefully. "She may be going to him."

But the bay mare was only taking her newly born filly away from the older foals. She knew the others played rough and her filly needed a few more days before she'd match them in strength. The mare came to a stop, then lowered her head to graze, never noticing the colt who stood such a short distance away from her.

The colt looked at her, but there was no sign of recognition, no attempt on his part to go to her. Instead, his head moved slightly in the direction of the others in the band. But he did not go to them either. Perhaps he was afraid. Perhaps he had no interest in them.

"The mare isn't going to take him," Pitch said. "He doesn't mean a thing to her. It's just as though he'd never been born to her. I never heard of such a thing." He paused, then added indignantly, "It's not right of her, Steve. It's not right. Let's get a rope, lasso her, tie her up and get the colt to her!"

"It wouldn't work," Steve said miserably. "We couldn't get a rope on a wild mare like her. And even if we did we couldn't get her to let the colt nurse, to accept him . . . unless she wanted to. And she doesn't want to."

Suddenly the foal's small tail moved with a jerk, and he shook his thin body.

"Flies," Steve said bitterly.

Pitch watched the other foals in the band making use of their mothers' sweeping tails as their protection against flying insects and he understood Steve's bitterness.

Flame trotted past the foal and went to the band. He encircled the mares, neighing repeatedly as though in reprimand. But he served only to frighten them and they moved farther up the valley.

Flame came back and stopped a few feet away from the colt. His long tail whisked the air, and for the first time the colt moved. Carefully he shuffled over the ground until he was beside the great stallion and making use of Flame's long tail to keep the flies off him.

"That's it," Pitch said. "His father's taken over."

"But Flame can't give him any milk," Steve pointed out. "He needs the mare for that."

"Yes, he needs . . ." Pitch stopped, then his voice rose excitedly. "But we've got milk, Steve! Lots of it!"

Quickly the boy turned to him. He'd never thought . . . In all the excitement it had never occurred to him that they had powdered whole milk, that they could give it to the foal, that perhaps they could keep him alive without the mare!

His excitement matched Pitch's. "Maybe we can. Maybe that's it!"

Together they ran to get the colt. Pitch picked him up without ever thinking that Flame might resent his hasty handling of the foal.

Steve took the colt's hindquarters, while Pitch picked up the fore. Carrying the colt in this way, they went down the valley at a fast walk, Flame following close behind.

Near the water pool, they set down their burden and ran up the trail. Arriving on the ledge, Pitch was the first to reach the tin of powdered milk. Excitedly he took it in his hands, turning it around to find the instructions on the back of the label.

"I know they use powdered milk in formulas for babies when they can't get bottled milk," he said, his words tumbling over one another.

"Take it easy, Pitch," Steve jibed. "Don't get so excited. You passed the instructions. They're on this side." He tried to steady the can in Pitch's hands, but he only succeeded in fumbling too.

"Who's excited? I'm not excited. Don't *you* get excited. Mrs. Reynolds—you know the Mrs. Reynolds I boarded with on your block, the one who had all the kids—well, when she went on an automobile trip she always took powdered milk instead of bottled milk so it wouldn't spoil."

"Here, Pitch . . . over here are the instructions. But it doesn't say anything about feeding babies."

"Where? Oh, yes. It's in Spanish, isn't it? '*Klim se produce removiendo solamente el aqua de la leche de vaca fresca y limpia.*'" He paused and looked up at Steve. "That says, 'Klim is made by removing the water from fresh, clean——'"

"'Pasteurized cow's whole milk,'" Steve finished for him. "It's all right here in English, Pitch, on the other side."

Pitch turned the can around to read the instructions in English. When he had finished he said, "You're right; it doesn't say anything about feeding babies. But to make regular whole milk that you've been drinking, it says to use eight tablespoonfuls to a pint of water."

"But we should cut that," Steve said quickly. "We shouldn't make it too rich for him."

"Right again," Pitch agreed. "So let's make it two tablespoonfuls to a pint of water, and see how he gets along on it."

"All right, Pitch, but let's hurry," Steve said impatiently. "Let's mix it and give it to him."

"But we can't do it just like that," Pitch returned, snapping his fingers.

"Why can't we? All we have to do is to put the powder in the water and mix it."

"But we can't. We have to sterilize everything first."

"*Sterilize?*" Steve asked incredulously.

"Yes, Steve," Pitch answered solemnly. "We're feeding a baby, and babies are very susceptible to disease."

"But there's no disease here, Pitch."

"We're not certain of that, Steve. There are germs almost everywhere. So I say we should boil the water, the jar and everything we're going to use." He paused, then shrugged his shoulders. "But I don't know anything about feeding a foal, Steve. If you know more about orphaned foals, or anything at all about their feeding, why speak up."

"No," Steve confessed. "I don't know a thing, Pitch."

"Then I feel that we should feed this foal just as we'd feed a baby until we find out otherwise from someone who does know. And I've watched Mrs. Reynolds feeding her babies and I know she sterilized everything. But he's your foal, Steve. I'll do as you say."

Steve cast a glance at the valley below. The colt was moving a little. Flame was a short distance away. Everything looked all right. The colt had waited this long for his milk; it probably wouldn't hurt him to wait just a little while longer. And Pitch was right. The only thing they could do for the time being was to feed this colt as they would a human baby. Perhaps sterilization wasn't necessary. But perhaps it was. They'd better do it, for there was no sense in taking any chances now.

"Okay, Pitch, let's sterilize," he said.

Pitch already had the stove going and the water was being heated. "We'll give everything a good boiling," he said.

Steve stooped down to help him. "I guess we've become foster mothers," he said quietly.

"Yes, I guess we have," Pitch agreed.

5

Red Fury

THE water was in a large aluminum kettle. After a while Pitch lifted the lid. "It's coming to a boil, Steve," he said, "and there's enough water to sterilize everything and make a gallon of milk formula for the colt."

"But we don't want him to drink a gallon at first," Steve said quickly. "I'd say give him a little, about a half-pint, at frequent intervals, maybe every hour."

"Yes, but we should make up a lot now, while we're at it," Pitch said. "Saves work. We can keep a gallon jug of milk in the pool, where it'll be kept cold and won't spoil."

Steve turned away from Pitch to look down at the foal in the valley. "But how will we get the milk into him, Pitch? We don't have any nursing nipples around, do we?"

"*Nipples?* Nursing nipples?" Pitch wearily shook his head. "I didn't know we were going to start a nursery here," he replied, and there was just a touch of sarcasm in his voice. Then he looked up at the boy,

59

smiled, and said more patiently, "Why can't we just pour it down his throat?"

"We couldn't, Pitch. He'd choke."

"Then maybe he'll just drink the milk from a pail."

"Maybe in a few days he could do that," Steve said, "but not now. He's too young; he couldn't be taught right away."

"Then what do *you* suggest?"

Steve was unable to make any answer at first. He knew Pitch was becoming impatient with him and the orphaned foal. Pitch's first love wasn't horses, as it was his. Although Pitch would do everything he could to help save the colt's life, he wanted to get back to his own work as soon as possible. He wanted to be relieved of all responsibility to this foal, and the sooner the better.

"I'll have to use a spoon," Steve said finally. "That's the only way I know to get the milk into him."

Pitch shrugged his shoulders. "A spoon it is, then."

The water in the kettle was boiling, but they left it on the fire until they felt certain all or any germs had been killed. Then they sterilized the utensils they were going to use in the feeding of the foal. There was enough water left over to fill the gallon jug which was to hold their milk formula.

"Now we have to wait for it to cool off before we add the powdered milk," Pitch said. "It mixes better."

"Can't I cool off the water right away?" Steve asked. "I'm worried about that colt. He's gone so long without food. I could cool it off in the stream."

"Yes, you can do that. But be careful that the glass doesn't break."

Taking the gallon jug, Steve ran up to the top of the waterfall; there he carefully cooled off the jug and then submerged it in the stream. While waiting for the sterile water inside to cool even more, he watched the foal. Flame had left him to rejoin his band, and the colt stood alone again. But he moved about more now, his long legs shuffling over the ground and taking him first in one direction, then in another. He stayed in the immediate vicinity of the water pool, seemingly having no desire to join the band that grazed far up the valley.

A feeling of pity for him swept over Steve. He'd do everything he possibly could to keep this foal alive!

When the sterile water was cool enough for the foal to drink, Steve returned to the ledge with it. He removed the cap of the jug, and Pitch put in eight tablespoonfuls of powdered milk.

"Let's put a spoonful of sugar in it, too," Steve said. "It can't do him any harm, and maybe he'll like it better."

That done, Steve replaced the cap and vigorously

shook the jug until the powder and sugar were well mixed with the water.

"That's enough," Pitch said. "Now let's pour whatever amount you're going to give him into this pint jar. It's been sterilized, too."

"We'll give him a half-pint," Steve said as Pitch poured.

When they reached the valley floor, Pitch placed the gallon jug in a corner of the water pool, where it would be kept cool and safe. Then he rejoined Steve as the boy approached the foal.

"You're going to eat," Steve told the colt, placing his hand on the soft nose and stroking it. "You'll like this, boy." Then, speaking to Pitch, "I guess we'd better get him down on the ground. It'll be easier."

"You get him down then," Pitch said. "I'll hold the milk."

Steve put his arms around the foal, fore and hind, then carefully placed him down on his side; the colt scarcely stirred.

"You hold him still now, Pitch," Steve said. "He just might struggle and upset the jar while I'm feeding him."

He knelt beside the small head, stroking it, talking to the colt all the while. The colt was too little, too weak to do any fighting. But the milk would come as a surprise to him. He could have no idea what they intended doing and perhaps he didn't care.

Steve raised the foal's head a little so that once the milk was in his mouth it would flow down his throat. Taking up a spoonful, he carefully opened the foal's mouth on the side and fed him the milk.

The foal struggled a little, even made an attempt to get up. But Pitch had no trouble keeping him down, and after a minute or two Steve gave him another spoonful of milk. There was less struggling by the foal this time. With the fourth spoonful he ceased

fighting altogether, taking the milk as readily and as often as Steve fed it to him.

Steve stopped when the foal had finished a quarter of a pint. "I think that's enough for him now," he told Pitch. "I'll give him that much every hour until I see how he reacts to it."

"Just as you say, Steve." Pitch stood up, releasing the colt. "But it's a full time job feeding him that often. And you'll have to sterilize the jar and spoon each time, as well as warm the milk."

"I know," Steve said. "But I'll be able to feed him alone after this. You won't have to help me."

"I *want* to help you," Pitch returned quietly.

The foal made no attempt to get to his feet. But his eyes were open, and there was a clearness to them that hadn't been there before. His breathing was better too, regular and without effort.

"I believe he's going to do all right on that formula," Pitch said, watching him. "He seems very contented now."

"The warm milk has probably made him sleepy," Steve said. "Rest and the sun will do him good."

They heard the beat of Flame's running hoofs and turned to watch the stallion as he came down the valley. He stopped beside Steve, but his eyes were only for the foal.

Steve put a hand on him. "I guess we've got someone to look after, Flame," he told the stallion. "And he's so little; he'll take a lot of care if we're going to do a good job."

Pitch let his gaze travel over the valley. "It would be so much better if we could only get the mare to let him nurse just once," he said. "Maybe she'd accept him as hers then. The cow's milk we're giving him is only a fair substitute for her milk. And he needs her care, too. Being any kind of an orphan is hard. And no matter how good we are to him, we're not going to take the place of his mother. It just isn't natural."

"But what can we do, Pitch?" Steve asked miserably. "Everything you say is true. But she's abandoned him, and we can't force her to take him back. By now she doesn't even remember having had him. I'm sure of that."

Flame tossed his head, and Steve rubbed the stallion's red coat hard in an attempt to rid himself of the anxiety which troubled him as much as it did Pitch.

"I still might be able to get a rope around her," Pitch suggested.

"But she's wild, just like all the others in the band," Steve said. "You wouldn't stand a chance of holding her."

"I could if I cut down one of those dwarfed trees over there and made a snubbing post of it," Pitch returned seriously. "I'd tie her fast, then we'd try and get the colt up to her."

"I doubt that we could do it," Steve said. "And if we did get her fast to the post, she might kick the devil out of the colt before she'd let him nurse her."

"But we might try, Steve. It's worth it as our last resort."

Steve glanced away from Pitch to the foal, who now had his eyes closed and was sleeping.

"All right, Pitch. It's worth a try, as you say. Anything to get him back to her!"

During the afternoon and early evening, Steve fed the colt every hour. Pitch offered to help, but Steve told him that it wasn't necessary, that the colt took the milk from him and gave no trouble. Actually it took a lot of patience and was hard work but never tedious, for the foal responded quickly to the life-giving milk. He was more alert, more active. And for Steve there was the wonderful satisfaction of having the colt come forward at sight of him, hungry and eager.

That evening Pitch said, "He's become so dependent on you in just one day that we'll have trouble getting him to the mare even if I do manage to get her tied fast."

"There's a difference, and he'll know it if she accepts him," Steve said, as he busied himself with the stove and the water he was boiling.

"You're not going to feed him every hour tonight, are you? You've got to sleep yourself, you know."

"I'll get up two or three times, I guess," Steve said. "He'll be all right. I'm giving him a little more milk during the night feedings."

Pitch watched Steve for a while, then said, "I have the post. I'll dig a hole for it in the morning, then we'll wait our chance to get a rope around the mare."

"All right, Pitch," Steve said without looking up.

The next morning Pitch dug his post hole not far from the water pool, figuring that the best opportunity to lasso the bay mare would be when she and the others came down to drink.

Steve fed the colt, marveling at what seemed to him to be more flesh on the frail, little body. He told himself that he might be wrong about the colt's added weight, but there was no doubt that the foal was stronger, more sure of himself on this, his second day. His eyes were no longer fuzzy and bewildered, but bright and clear. He watched Steve's every move, staying close and only leaving him when Flame came down the valley to join them. But he would never follow Flame when the stallion returned to the band. Instead, he would always turn away from him, looking again for Steve.

Pitch finished putting up the post, and called Steve over to examine it.

"It's solid," Pitch said, his hand on the post. "It'll hold the mare, all right, if I get her tied to it."

Simultaneously their eyes strayed to the band far up the valley. "They should be coming down in a little while for water," Pitch said. "And you know, Steve, I got thinking last night that it might be wise if we put the foal in Bottle Canyon at night. The youngsters in the band might hurt him when they come down to the pool. They're much stronger than he is."

"I watched them last night," Steve said. "Flame wouldn't let any of them come near him. But you're right, Pitch. We could easily do that, then if Flame should be away from him when the band comes down at night we'll be sure that no harm can come to him."

"That's what I thought. I cut down a couple of thin trees to make rails which we can put across the entrance to the canyon. That'll keep him in nights and the others out."

Steve looked at the post. "But if we get the mare tied and the colt to her, we won't need to do that."

"No," Pitch agreed, "of course not."

Pitch returned to the ledge, while Steve went to the foal. The soft nose nuzzled his hand, searching for milk.

"You just had it," Steve told him. "You've got another hour to go before you get any more." He could feel the soft gums of the colt's mouth as the foal pulled at his fingers. He looked into the eyes set far apart in the wide forehead and saw the mischievous light in them as the colt held on to his fingers. Then his gaze traveled to the long, delicate nostrils now partly closed but ready to open wide at any movement he might make to get his hand free. This foal was so much Flame's colt, every bit of him. He was small, perhaps much smaller than any of the other foals had been at birth. But then he was a twin, and his sister was just as small. He would grow to be tall and strong just as she would. Or would he, without the mare's milk?

Steve turned to look at the band. He loved the foal, loved caring for him, but he would help Pitch in every way to rope the mare and make her accept her son. To grow big and strong, the colt needed her. Certainly no cow's milk could take the place of hers. And he, Steve, couldn't be expected to do as good a job of caring for him as could the mare. As Pitch had said, it just wasn't natural.

Steve saw the band start down the valley. "Pitch!" he yelled. "They're coming!"

A few minutes later Pitch was beside him. In his hand he carried a long rope.

"Let's take the colt to Bottle Canyon," Pitch

said. "We can get him again if we succeed in getting the mare tied to the post. Meanwhile, it'll keep him out of the way."

The foal struggled as they picked him up. He was stronger, there was no doubt of that. But without too much trouble they were able to carry him across the valley to the mouth of Bottle Canyon. Putting him just inside, they placed long rails across the entrance.

"It's not a very sturdy gate," Pitch said, wedging the ends of the rails between the stones. "But it'll hold him in all right."

They went back near the pool and awaited the coming of the band.

"Don't get any closer," Pitch warned. "We'll only frighten them away."

"They're not all coming down," Steve said. "Just a small group of them."

"Is she with them . . . the bay mare?"

"I can't tell yet. Five of the mares are bay. They're all too far away."

"Look for the twin filly," Pitch said, fingering the rope. "You ought to recognize the mare by the filly at her side. She's smaller than the others."

"All the foals are too close to the mares to tell yet."

They waited while the small group of mares stopped to graze, then came on again. "They're after water. They'll be down, all right. Can you see her, Steve?"

"I think so, but I'm not sure."

The mares stopped to graze again. Steve looked past them at the main part of the band farther up the valley. He saw Flame far beyond, grazing alone. Steve glanced sideways at the barred canyon on his right; the foal was at the gate, watching, waiting.

"That noose," Steve said, referring to the rope Pitch was fingering so nervously. "Have you fixed it so it won't run too tight around her neck?"

"It's knotted. It'll hold her without choking her." Pitch's words were tense, clipped, for the group of mares had moved toward them again. "That's her, isn't it, Steve? See that filly! She went right under the mare's belly to get away from that gray foal!"

"Yes," Steve said, "that's the mare, all right."

"Don't move, Steve. Don't move!"

"I'm not moving."

Steve knew that Pitch was very nervous, even frightened. He'd had no experience roping any kind of a horse, let alone a wild mare. But he was going through with his plan just the same.

"I'll throw the rope if you want," Steve said. But he knew he had no better chance of roping the mare than Pitch. And he was just as nervous.

"No. No, I'll do it," Pitch said. "But we'll move together, and if I should get it around her, Steve . . .

if I should, why . . ." He stopped, turning to Steve, and a white pallor showed beneath his tanned skin. "W-what do we do then?"

"We get our end of the rope around the post," Steve said.

"Yes, and then we'll pull her to it until she's fast."

Steve nodded in agreement. But it wasn't until the mares were close to the pool and he and Pitch took a step forward that Steve wondered how they were going to pull the mare fast to the post. She was ever so much stronger than they were. He was about to ask Pitch about it when the latter put a hand across his lips.

"S-Shh, Steve."

The boy followed close behind Pitch, feeling very strongly that what they were trying to do was foolish, even insane. But the foal needed his dam, and this knowledge drove Steve on, the same as it did Pitch.

They were close against the wall. The drone of the waterfall silenced their footsteps. There was no wind to carry their scent to the mares. They were near the pool now . . . not far from the bay mare. She was within reach of the rope.

Pitch's body tensed, and Steve guessed he would throw the rope as soon as the mare finished drinking, as soon as she straightened and turned in their direction. There was no doubt but that she would do just that, for the other mares were too close on her right for her to turn toward them.

"Relax, Pitch," Steve wanted to say. "If you're tense your aim won't be true." But he said nothing. They were too close to the mares.

Pitch held the noose in his right hand, ready to throw. Steve saw the twin filly move quickly around the bay mare. They'd have to be careful not to hurt the filly. It would be terrible if they caused her any injury in their efforts to help the colt. He'd better caution Pitch to . . .

The bay mare straightened. There was the quick but jerky movement of Pitch's arm. The noose struck the mare on the side of her neck instead of dropping over her head! Neighing shrilly, the bay mare twirled; then the whole group was in motion, getting into one another's way in their frenzy to escape this sudden danger.

Pitch had run forward. He was drawing up the rope, getting ready to throw again. Steve stared after him. The mares' confusion afforded Pitch still another chance.

But as he followed Pitch he heard Flame's shrill whistle, then the terrible pounding of hoofs. He looked beyond to find the stallion only fifty yards away *and charging Pitch!*

He screamed to Pitch and Flame in the same

breath. Pitch saw the oncoming stallion, turned and started back, then fell.

Flame came on, his ears back, his nostrils spread wide in his fury. Steve shouted again, but the stallion had reached Pitch. Flame stopped before the man's

inert body. He pawed the ground but his pounding hoofs never touched Pitch. Steve ran forward.

He reached for his friend with trembling hands, pulling him to his feet. Then they just stood there, terrified in their knowledge of what Flame could do with hoofs and teeth when enraged.

Steve tried to find the words to say to Flame. But they wouldn't come. The stallion had seen Pitch chasing the mares, *his mares*, and he had seen the rope. It had been enough to send his hot blood raging and to fill his mind with only one thought: *to protect his band*. But he had not killed. Something had stopped him: his recognition of Pitch, Steve's screams, or the sudden realization that Pitch actually meant no harm to his mares.

Pitch stood close beside Steve, one hand on the boy's arm. Slowly the pounding in his heart lessened. Slowly reassurance came to him that he was no longer in any great danger with Steve at his side. He heard Steve's voice. The boy was talking to the stallion, and his words were soft, caressing. As Pitch listened, his eyes remained on Flame. He saw the spreading nostrils begin to close, the fury begin to ebb from the giant body. He marveled at what he saw and heard. He forgot his fear, forgot everything else in witnessing Steve's domination of this untamed stallion.

Once before, the previous year when they had found Blue Valley, he had heard Steve talk this way to Flame. During the ensuing weeks he had come to accept Steve's mastery of the stallion as a matter of course. Only now, though, did he accept this relationship between boy and horse for what it actually was.

Not that he understood it. No person could say truthfully he understood why or how a boy could still a wild rage like the one that filled this stallion. And Pitch wasn't even going to try to understand it.

He listened to Steve's words coming so soft and with a kind of rhythm. Few people in the world could talk that way to a horse . . . to any animal. The sound and words were those of a mother talking to her child; it was the only comparison Pitch knew. Soft words, sentimental words. Many adults would laugh if they heard them. Sickly sentimentalism, they would say, never knowing or understanding that the words came from the heart of a boy who loved this horse.

And there were still other adults, men like Tom, for example, who went further than ridiculing such caressing words, such soft and gentle touches as Steve now gave Flame. They would say, as he'd heard Tom say very often, *There's only one way to conquer a wild horse. You've got to break him with your own hands. You've got to show him who's boss!*

But they'd never seen what he'd seen. They

weren't watching Steve now . . . Steve and Flame.

The boy was standing beside the stallion, his hand on the arched neck. There was nothing frightening about Flame now. He was quiet, docile, allowing Steve to straighten his mane, his forelock.

"Pitch. Come over."

The man's footsteps lagged and he was extremely cautious when he did come. He'd rather have kept away from the stallion, have left it all up to Steve. But the boy wanted him to come. Perhaps Steve was right. Perhaps it would be best to make friends again now.

He stopped beside the boy. He touched the stallion with nervous, careful fingertips. Nothing happened. Flame turned his head in the direction of the band, but that was all. Pitch rested the palm of his hand on the stallion's back, then he stroked him, slowly, carefully. He knew everything was all right again. But he was lucky. He could have been killed. Never again would he chase any of the mares in Flame's band. No . . . never, never again.

6

Sea Entrance

THAT evening Steve was preparing to leave the ledge for his eight o'clock feeding of the foal when Pitch said, "I thought I'd go to Antago sometime tomorrow morning, Steve."

"You need to go?"

"I want to check with the vet about our feeding of the colt. I might as well do it now as later."

"He seems to be doing very well on what I'm giving him, Pitch. I'm sure we can wait until you have to go to Antago for supplies or something, then you won't have to make any extra trips." Steve knew how much Pitch wanted to get back to his explorations and manuscript. The trip to Antago would take away from him another full day of work, and Steve felt guilty about it.

"I'd rather do it now than have it on my mind," Pitch said. "Besides, we need more powdered milk. It's going fast."

Steve looked into the almost empty can. "Don't

you have more in the chamber, where you keep the extra supplies? I thought I saw some there."

"No. But there's a small can in the launch. You can get that tomorrow morning and it'll hold you over until I get back."

"Okay, Pitch." Steve reached for the tablespoon which he had been sterilizing in boiling water.

Watching him, Pitch said, "Maybe the vet will say all this sterilization isn't necessary. It'll save you a lot of work, if it isn't. And I'll bring back some nursing nipples; they'll be easier than using a spoon."

Steve nodded, then suddenly thought of something. "But what will you tell the vet, Pitch? I mean, how much will you tell him? What if he asks you, *where is this orphaned foal?*"

"I don't think he will, Steve. I don't know him very well, and I'll just be seeking information for a friend of mine." Pitch smiled. "You're a friend of mine." Pausing, he added, "But even if he does pin me down I'll tell him the foal is on Azul Island and he'll think only of the band on the spit. And I won't be lying, for the colt *is* on Azul Island."

"But you'd better be careful," Steve warned.

"I will. You can count on me for that," Pitch replied. "I don't want anyone to suspect what we've found any more than you do."

When Steve went down to the valley floor, he

heard the colt before he was able to see him in the dim light of the starlit valley. A soft neigh came to him, then the sound of a slight movement of hoofs. Steve saw the outline of the foal's figure as he came trotting across the valley. And he marveled that while yesterday the foal could hardly move about, tonight he was trotting! Tomorrow he might even take his first few strides at a run!

The colt stopped before him, his muzzle seeking the glass jar he had come to know so well. It was no longer necessary for Steve to put him on the ground to feed him. He had only to hold the colt's head steady and spoon the milk into his eager mouth. Tonight he counted the number of spoonfuls in the half-pint of milk he gave the foal. He stopped counting when he had reached thirty and there was more milk still left in the jar. Pitch was right; it was going to be a lot easier feeding the colt when they had nursing nipples.

Finally the jar was empty, and Steve straightened, relaxing his cramped back muscles. He watched the foal bend his long forelegs in an attempt to reach the grass. Successful in pulling loose a few blades, the colt held them between his lips without trying to chew them. He had no taste for grass yet, that would come later.

Steve ran his hands over the hardening body and down the legs to the tiny, fawn-like hoofs. He handled the foal this way every hour, rubbing him to strengthen the muscles and to stimulate circulation. He picked up each foot to get the foal used to his holding them. Already Steve had begun the early training of this colt which so completely relied upon him, belonged to him.

And now he thought of the other things he would ask Pitch to bring back in order that he might continue this early training. A small, soft brush to groom the colt. He had one he used on Flame, but it was too large and heavy for the foal's slight body. And a soft web halter, too, which the colt could wear. It would make it easier to train him to be led, to stand still, to be tied.

This early schooling was very important, for Steve was determined that when he left for home he was going to take the colt with him. He told himself that he had to do it because the colt would be relying on him for milk for at least six months, and therefore the only thing he could do was to take him home. Actually Steve had his own reasons for wanting to take the colt with him. The colt would be living evidence of the lost world within the walls of Azul Island. The colt would help him through the long months when he would be away from Blue Valley and Flame. Steve knew he'd never be able to take Flame away from the island, for the great stallion belonged there with his band. But the colt didn't belong. He was an orphan, an outcast even from this forsaken band.

The boy reached down to lift the foal, and carried him the short distance to Bottle Canyon.

Early the next morning Steve was back to turn the colt loose in Blue Valley and to feed him again. He left the colt stretched out asleep in the sun after the meal, and went back below the ledge.

"Pitch!" he shouted.

"Yes, Steve?" Pitch looked down.

"I'm going to the launch for the can of powdered milk. Please keep your eye on the colt if the band comes down for water."

"All right, Steve. I'll be ready to leave in about an hour or so. I'm just finishing some work."

Steve walked part way up the valley, then whistled to Flame when he saw the stallion emerging from the cane. There came a quickening beat to Flame's running hoofs, then he was in full gallop.

He neared Steve with flying mane and tail, his sharply pointed ears pricked forward and almost touching at the tips. He plunged past, then came to a sudden stop, whirled, and returned to the boy, stopping at his side.

His action free and graceful, Flame pranced at Steve's side. The boy put his hands on the stallion, then quickly pulled himself up. Hardly did he have his balance when Flame was off with giant strides.

Faster and faster the long legs moved, and Steve shifted his weight forward.

He kept Flame far to the left of where the band was grazing and finally sent him flying into the tall cane, never slowing the stallion's strides until they came out on the other side of the field. Before them now was the long, gradual climb to the base of the western wall of the valley.

Without any direction from Steve, Flame turned to the right, running between the field of cane and the wall. He seemed to know where they were going. Less than a mile away, a thin cloud of vapor was beginning to rise from the hollow which fostered the marsh.

The footing beneath Flame's running feet was hard and stony, so Steve kept the stallion at a slow canter lest he stumble and fall. He slowed him down still more when they reached the rim of the hollow and started their descent. The ground became soft, and voluntarily Flame slowed to a walk as he neared the edge of the swamp.

The foul smell of rotting vegetation was in their nostrils, but Steve knew the odor wasn't anything compared to what it would be when the vapors thickened with the heat of the noonday sun. Flame's hoofs made soft sucking sounds as he went toward one of the narrow green avenues running through the marsh.

At a very slow walk the stallion entered the cloud-like world, following hoofprints which he had left from countless other journeys. He was no stranger to the marsh. Solid ground was beneath his feet, but on either side was a slimy wilderness of high reeds, swamp ferns and all-engulfing quagmires.

Steve hated this place, but he made no attempt to hurry Flame. A slip, a fall a few feet on either side meant a terrible death in the still, black pools. But while the marsh was long it wasn't wide and he knew they'd be out of it within a few minutes. They were going in the direction of the western wall. Steve looked straight ahead, toward the high cut that shattered the wall. He thought of the name Pitch had given it on his map—Dry Stream Gorge. Well, that's exactly what it was, for a stream had once cut that gorge and had flowed into the hollow. It was now dry because the Conquistadores had diverted the stream in order to use this gorge as a passage to Blue Valley. At least, that's what he and Pitch had decided between them.

They emerged from the marsh and Flame began his climb up the twisting, turning gorge. High yellow walls rose on either side of them, and the way was strewn with stones and boulders. Flame attempted to lengthen his strides, but Steve kept him at a slow walk, fearing he might fall and injure himself.

At the top of the gorge the yellow walls widened. Set amidst their towering peaks was the green sliver of a long and narrow valley.

Steve stopped a moment to rest Flame. "On the map Pitch calls this Small Valley," he said aloud. Nothing fancy about any of the names Pitch had given these places. But then there was nothing fancy about Pitch, either. Smiling, Steve led Flame into the valley.

The far wall toward which he rode was split with many chasms and caves. From one cave flowed a stream which came a short way down the valley, then turned suddenly and disappeared at the base of the northern wall. It was this stream which had been diverted from flowing into the hollow in Blue Valley.

When he reached the stream, Steve slid off Flame's back to let the stallion drink. The far wall was only a hundred yards away, and he intended to go the rest of the way alone, leaving Flame to graze.

He hurried toward the chasm just to the right of the cave from which the stream came. With no hesitation he entered it. The sea entrance to Azul Island was just a short distance away. Already he could hear the dull thud of the waves beating against the outer wall.

At the end of the chasm loomed a large hole. Steve stopped for a moment to accustom his eyes to the dim, gray light. Then he hurried on, bracing himself against the gusts of wind that intermittently came at him.

Fine white sand was beneath his feet, and as Steve rounded a turn the light became brighter. Then he stepped into the great rectangular chamber that housed the entrance to the sea. Through the center of the chamber ran a narrow canal, its waters flooding and ebbing with the waves which struck the outer wall and found their way inside through a low but wide hole at the base.

Steve went to the motor launch that was moored to one of the low, moss-covered piles on the side of the canal. Boarding, he found the can of powdered milk which Pitch had left in the galley. He looked around the launch for anything else he might need. But the only things to be seen were a pile of rope in the stern and two more picks.

Before leaving, he turned to look at the great wooden panels above the sea hole. The two panels could be slid apart, giving the hole in the wall all the height anyone would need to bring in a launch. But unless one knew about it one would never suspect the existence of the false partition from the sea, for outside it was the color of the walls, and the hole itself was too low for anyone to notice.

It was through this entrance that the Conquistadores had brought their men, their weapons, and their horses to Blue Valley. Steve thought of them now, wondering what it would have been like to have been one of them. Then his thoughts turned back to Flame and Pitch and the foal. He'd better return to Blue Valley, for Pitch probably was ready to leave for Antago.

He hurried from the chamber without a backward glance.

Later, when he rode Flame into the dry stream gorge leading back to the marsh, he slowed down the stallion reluctantly. He was anxious to get back to Blue Valley, more anxious and worried than he should have been. And there wasn't any reason for it, he told himself. No reason at all. He hadn't been gone more than an hour. Pitch was taking care of the foal. Nothing could have happened. Pitch wouldn't let the colt out of his sight. He could depend upon that. Yet his uneasiness that something had gone wrong during his short absence persisted. There was nothing to account for it, yet try as he did he couldn't rid himself of it.

He started to urge Flame out of his cautious walk around the stones of the gorge, then stopped himself from giving any command to the stallion. He couldn't risk going faster. Flame knew this twisting, turning gorge, and he was going down it carefully. To increase his speed might result in a broken leg.

Just the thought of it caused Steve to sit back and try again to relax.

They were almost at the end of the gorge. Another turn would take them to the marsh and after that they'd be in Blue Valley. He'd let Flame go at full gallop then, Steve decided.

The stallion slipped as they made the last sharp turn, regained his balance and went on. Steve was giving thanks to Flame's sure-footedness when he saw the foal.

The colt was lying sprawled on the jagged stones.

Flame snorted. Beyond the colt, emerging from the marsh, was Pitch. He looked at them, then at the foal. "He followed you," Pitch called, running toward the colt. "I tried, but I couldn't keep up with him."

Steve slid off Flame's back, his heart like lead, his stomach sick.

7

Forced Journey

THE foal raised his head as Steve neared him. He uttered a short neigh, then lowered his head again. His eyes were clear; there was no pain in them.

Steve turned to Pitch, who now stood beside him. "Maybe he's just tired," he said hopefully.

"Could be," Pitch said, the fear gone from his voice, too. "He's been going a long time for him, ever since you and Flame started up the valley. He watched you a moment, then got to his feet and went into that mincing trot of his. I yelled, but he paid no attention to me so I started after him. He stopped often to rest, but whenever I was just about to get my hands on him he'd start moving again. He went right past the band—scarcely even noticed them. I guess he didn't want to forget which way you and Flame had gone. Four times I almost caught him before he reached the marsh, but he always got away. And how he ever found his way through the marsh, I'll never know. Maybe he followed Flame's hoof-prints. Maybe it was only instinct which showed him the way. He was a good two hundred yards ahead of me by that time, I guess."

Pitch turned to look at the foal before adding, "You know as much about what happened after that as I do. I was just coming out of the marsh when you and Flame appeared. The colt could be exhausted and just resting now . . . or he could have stumbled and fallen. I don't know, Steve. I'm sorry it had to happen, but I did my best to catch him."

The boy was bending over the foal. "Come on, fellow. Let's get up now." The colt nuzzled him, pulling his fingers. It was an encouraging sign. "I think he's just resting, Pitch. He doesn't seem to be in any pain."

"No, he doesn't."

The colt was lying on his right side, his legs outstretched. There was no mark on him, no apparent evidence of injury. But Steve saw the large boulder a few feet behind the colt. If the colt had struck that on his way up the gorge, he could have fallen hard and be hurt without their knowing it.

"Let's try to get him up, Pitch. If he stands without showing any sign of pain we'll know he's all right."

Flame had been watching them from a few feet away, but now he came close to the foal, nickering and stretching his neck toward him.

Steve got his hands around the foal's shoulders,

while Pitch took the hindquarters. "Easy now," Steve said, addressing both the foal and Pitch. A startled expression came into the colt's eyes, but he did not struggle. "We just want you to stand a minute, fellow, then you can rest again," Steve told him.

The colt's long legs were under him. With great care Steve and Pitch kept their hands on him when the tiny hoofs touched the ground. They sent worried glances at the legs which supported the tired, wavering body. The forelegs were unsteady but down, so were the hind. *No!* The colt wasn't using his right hind leg to support any of his weight!

Steve dropped down beside him, sick at heart again. Feeling, probing, he ran his hand down the foal's leg. Only after he had passed the hock did he feel anything.

"Pitch!"

The colt tried to move away on three legs when Pitch dropped down beside Steve.

"Right here!" Steve said.

The man's fingers went to the leg, and the foal whinnied at his touch.

"Something's wrong," Pitch said gravely after a minute. "But maybe it's not a break . . . just a sprain."

"We've got to get him out of here. To the vet's, Pitch."

"You don't think that if we just wrapped it well, it'd heal?"

Steve shook his head, his eyes closed. "Not if we ever want him to use that leg again," he said miserably.

"But of course we want him to use it," Pitch returned quickly. "We'll take him to the veterinarian now, Steve. Right now," he repeated.

With grave faces they rose to their feet. Flame seemed to sense something was wrong for he stood without moving, without any sign of restlessness, just waiting.

"We'll have to carry him, Pitch."

The man nodded, but then he saw Flame and asked, "Can't you ride Flame and carry the foal in front of you? It would be easier on him and us."

A few minutes later Steve was on Flame, and Pitch was carefully lifting the foal up to him. They got the forelegs on one side of Flame, the hind legs on the other. Finally they started up the gorge, Pitch walking beside Flame and keeping one hand on the foal to help Steve hold him steady.

The going was hard in the gorge, but much easier in the small valley. They traveled faster up the valley and entered the chasm, not stopping until they came to the cave which led to the sea chamber. Only then did they speak again.

"Should we carry the foal from here?" Pitch asked.

"No, he's resting comfortably. It'll be easier if we go on as we are."

They entered the dimly lit cave and Flame walked carefully as though fully aware of the burden he carried. Never did he crabstep or break from his smooth, easy walk in the cave's white sand.

They came to the sea chamber and stopped beside the motor launch.

"We'll have to be careful getting him down now," Pitch cautioned. "I'll get his hindquarters and watch the leg. You just take care of him up front."

Flame never moved as Steve carefully raised the colt's forelegs, while Pitch lowered the hindquarters. Finally Pitch had the foal in his arms and was carrying him aboard the launch. Steve followed, and they placed the colt on a blanket in the stern. They stepped back to see if he would make any attempt to get to his feet. He didn't. He was weary and his eyes were half closed.

"At least he doesn't seem to be in pain," Steve said hopefully.

"He's probably too tired to feel anything just now," Pitch said. "And we were careful not to jostle him. But the sooner we get him to the vet the better. When he wakes up it might be different."

Steve was with Flame when Pitch started the

launch's motor. The roar of it caused the stallion to move quickly away. Steve watched him until he disappeared through the cave on his way back to Blue Valley, then he boarded the moving launch. The foal had raised his head a little at the sudden noise, but now was sleeping again. Steve hurried to the bow of the ship. Pitch kept the launch steady while Steve reached for the handholds in the wooden doors above the low sea hole. The partitions spread apart, sliding easily in their grooves.

"That's wide enough," Pitch yelled over the motor's roar. The wind swept into the chamber. The open sea was before them.

While Pitch was taking the launch through the exit, Steve ran back to the stern. Once they were outside the wall, Pitch held the boat steady while Steve closed the panels. Then he went to sit beside the foal. Pitch gunned the motor, taking the launch safely through a channel which found its way past the black shadows of submerged rocks.

It would take them about four hours to get to Antago, Steve knew. That meant it would be a little after noon when they arrived. He turned to look back at the yellow dome of Azul Island when they were well away from the barrier walls; then his gaze swept back to the foal, who still slept. The boat rocked on the swells of the open sea; there were no waves to speak of and the colt wouldn't be jostled in any way. Steve thought of the hours he had spent dreaming of taking this colt away with him from Blue Valley. *But not like this.* Would it be possible for the veterinarian to help him? Would it . . .

Steve got to his feet and joined Pitch at the wheel. He needed Pitch's assurance that everything would turn out all right.

"Even if it's a break, the vet on Antago could set it, couldn't he?"

"I've heard that he's a very good man, Steve." Pitch turned to the boy, saw the fear in his eyes, then added emphatically, "I'm certain everything will turn out all right. Bone injuries heal fast in the young. Why, Mrs. Reynolds' baby fell out of her high chair when she was only a year old and broke her collarbone. And new bone started forming within a few days!"

"I hope you're right."

"I *know* I'm right," Pitch said. "You'd better stop worrying about what the vet will do and start thinking about having some milk ready for the colt when he wakes up."

"I hadn't even thought of it, Pitch. Why, I don't have . . ."

"Yes, we do," the man said. "Go below to the galley and you'll find everything you need. The powdered milk is in the tin container marked 'Tea.' There's not much but it's enough for a couple of feedings until we get to Antago."

Pitch waited until the boy had disappeared down the short steps to the galley, then his face sobered and concern was evident in his eyes. He wasn't worried about the colt. He sincerely believed all he'd told Steve. It was his stepbrother Tom who was worrying him. If Tom had returned to Antago, if he by any wild chance saw the colt, all the strange things that had been happening during the last six months might be brought to a head. And it wouldn't be a happy affair. He had avoided telling Steve very much about Tom whenever the boy had asked. But now . . . now it would be best if Steve were told. They had to be ready for anything Tom might do if he did see them and the colt.

Later, Steve reappeared. "I found everything," he said. "I'm waiting for the water to cool." He turned to the foal, saw he was still sleeping, then asked, "Want me to take the wheel for a while, Pitch?"

"No, Steve . . . thanks." Pitch kept his eyes on the sea ahead. "Steve?"

"Yes, Pitch?"

"You've asked me about Tom several times since your return."

"Yes? What about him, Pitch?"

"I'd felt it best all along not to discuss Tom with you," Pitch said. "We were safe from him in Blue Valley. But now that you and the colt are going to

Antago . . ." He stopped as though to collect his thoughts, then plunged into what he had to say.

"Tom's been acting very strange the last five or six months. He's always been a domineering person, as you know. But it's more than that now. With no just cause, he's been cruel, even vicious at times, to the native help we've had at the plantation. Finally it reached the point where no one living on Antago would work for him. He lost our last cane crop. But even this didn't seem to bother him. I made it a point to keep out of his way. That wasn't very difficult for me to do, especially since he started making trips to the islands south of Antago and once even went to South America.

"While he was gone, I was able to get the natives back to work. But when Tom returned they'd leave again the moment they saw him. A week before you arrived, Tom left Antago once more, this time telling me he'd be in South America for a year."

When Pitch had finished, Steve studied his face a long while before asking, "Do you think he really went to South America, Pitch?"

"I don't know, Steve. He'd been restless and wanted excitement which he couldn't get on Antago. He'd lived there for years, longer than he'd ever settled down in any one place before. He could have gone to South America again but . . ." Pitch stopped.

"But what, Pitch? What makes you think he didn't?"

"The morning of the day you arrived a friend of mine told me he thought he'd seen the *Sea Queen* in the waters to the north."

Steve's gaze never left Pitch as they stood at the bow in silence. *Sea Queen* was the name of Tom's motor launch. If Tom had been going to South America he would have traveled west . . . to one of the western islands, where he could get a plane for South America.

"You think then," Steve said, "that he'd been to Azul Island? Does he have any idea what we've found there?"

"I don't honestly know, Steve. He may be curious about my trips to the spit to do a little excavation work. He knows of my interest in the island. But he didn't seem to take any active interest in my work until the last few months. In his sarcastic way he asked if my digging had turned up anything. I told him I'd found nothing on the spit . . . which I hadn't, of course."

"But why his sudden interest?" Steve asked gravely.

"Perhaps his restlessness was the cause of it. Perhaps it was your letters."

"You didn't let him see them, Pitch?" Steve's words were clipped.

"No, but I burned them after reading them. Tom saw me burning one. He probably guessed my only reason for doing such a thing was to keep the letter out of his hands. I should have been more careful."

They said nothing more for a long while, then Steve spoke. "And you're afraid he might have returned to Antago by this time? You're afraid he'll see the . . ."

". . . the colt." Pitch said it for him. "And if he did he'd know we *had* found something on Azul Island we were keeping to ourselves."

"But the colt could be from the band on the spit," Steve said quickly. "We can tell Tom that, if he sees us."

"But would he believe us?" Pitch asked quietly.

Steve turned to the foal, who was starting to wake up. Again he took note of the fine wedge-shaped head, the delicate lines of neck and body.

Even as he looked at the colt, Pitch reminded him, "Tom's been around horses most of his life. He'll see what you see, Steve . . . he'll know that that foal could never have been born from the stock on the spit."

The boy turned to him. "But we don't need to go to the plantation, do we, Pitch?"

"No. I did all I could there before your arrival. I have no reason to go."

"Then after we've seen the vet we'll go right back to Blue Valley," Steve said.

"Yes," Pitch agreed, "that's our best bet. Do what we have to do, then get off Antago fast." He paused. "I feel much better now that I've told you everything, Steve . . . much better."

The foal was fully awake, and Steve hurried below to the galley to get the milk for him.

During the remainder of the trip to Antago, Steve stayed with the colt, keeping him down on the blanket. There was pain in the foal's eyes now and Steve tried to comfort him, soothing him with voice and hands. Occasionally the foal would drop off to sleep again and only then would the boy's thoughts turn to Tom Pitcher and what he had seen this giant of a man do with the long bull whip which he wore wrapped around his bulging waist. He knew the terror Tom would bring to Blue Valley if he ever found the lost band of horses that grazed there.

But never would Tom find them. Never!

It was almost a year since Steve had last seen Tom Pitcher. But it could have been only an hour ago, for it wasn't easy to forget him. Steve saw his dark, low-jowled face with its beady, suspicious eyes always watching, waiting to catch one off guard. And when the opportunity came, Tom attacked viciously by word or action, for it was in him always to demonstrate his superiority over man and animal. Steve wondered now what instinct fostered Tom's determination to dominate everything before him. Was it fear? Was it pride in his tremendous body and strength? Anyway, it was there for anyone to see.

Steve thought again of the bull whip which Tom could use so skillfully that it might as well be his own arms going out to grasp and tear at will. Steve had seen him use it last summer.

There had been no escape for the small, wiry horse in the plantation's corral. Tom had run him before the whip until the horse could hardly stand. He'd fought him for what seemed to Steve to be a terrible love of fighting. And when the horse had stood before him with swaying and trembling body, Tom had regretted the end of the fight. Then the animal had been broken to saddle by Tom, broken in body by Tom, broken in spirit by Tom.

The colt moved, seeking to get to his feet. Steve quieted him, keeping his hands on the small, hard body, comforting him, protecting him.

Before noon they were within sight of Antago. The island lay green and rolling with no hill more than a hundred feet high. They could see the red-roofed homes which dotted the coastline and, beyond, the waving green fields of sugar cane. A half-hour later they rounded a point and came into Chestertown, the only port and town of any size on Antago.

A freighter was just off shore, transporting its cargo

into large, deep rowboats. But Pitch and Steve were more interested in the sailboats and launches moored to the wharf.

"Would the *Sea Queen* be here, if Tom's on Antago?" Steve asked from where he sat with the colt.

"Usually he keeps it here," Pitch said without turning around. "But he has a pier near the plantation also, and once in a while he uses that."

The foal raised his head as though he, too, wanted to know what lay ahead. Keeping the tiny body still, Steve said, "Quiet, fellow. Just be patient a little longer, and we'll have you at the doctor's."

Pitch said, "The *Sea Queen's* not here."

A few minutes later he brought the launch in to the end of the wharf, where he had left his car when he and Steve had set out for Azul Island a few days earlier. Steve helped him moor the boat, then they carried the foal to the car. There was plenty of activity going on farther down the wharf, near the great warehouse sheds, so scarcely anyone noticed their burden.

"You get in back with him," Pitch said. "That's it. But watch his legs; they're hitting the door."

They got the foal inside the car, stretched out on the seat. "It's the best we can do, Pitch," Steve said. "I'll watch his leg so it won't be jarred."

The man nodded and got behind the wheel. Leaving the long wharf, they went up the main street of

Chestertown. The noise and confusion were startling after the quiet of Blue Valley, and Steve tried to shut his eyes and ears to the sight and sound of the crazy tangle of traffic.

The shops on either side of the street were colorless but neat. The too-narrow sidewalks overflowed with busy people who spilled into the cobblestone road and scurried before cars and bicycles. They were predominantly Negro, and a few made their way through the bustling traffic skillfully balancing huge baskets on their heads. Native policemen, snappily dressed in khaki uniforms and caps, stood at the street intersections frantically blowing their whistles in an attempt to maintain some semblance of order.

Soon they had left the business section behind and were in the suburbs of Chestertown. Here they passed small, neat houses with yards of colorful tropical shrubs protected by freshly painted white fences.

"The vet's office is just a little farther on," Pitch said. "We'll soon be there."

They were out of the heaviest traffic when Steve noticed Pitch's frequent glances in the rear-view mirror. "What is it?" he asked.

"I thought I saw Tom's car behind us. But I must have been mistaken; it's not there now."

A mile farther on Pitch came to a stop before a two-story frame house. On the picket gate was the sign: "DR. F. A. MASON, **Veterinary**—Surgery and Medicine."

They carried the foal around the house to a low one-story building in the back. "Now let's just hope he's in," Pitch said, ringing the office bell.

A moment later, a bald-headed man appeared at the screen door. He had a gray mustache and a short, pointed beard.

"Dr. Mason?" Pitch asked.

"Yes," said the man, his eyes on the foal. "Bring him in," he said abruptly, holding the door open. "Follow me, please."

He ushered them into a large room with a tanbark floor. Another man, younger than Dr. Mason, looked up inquiringly as they approached. "This is Dr. Crane, my assistant."

"It's his leg," Steve said, ". . . his right hind."

Dr. Mason nodded. "Let Dr. Crane hold him, please. And step back from the table, if you will."

Pitch drew Steve away, but not before the boy had explained, "He fell, Doctor. He's hurt just below the hock."

"He can find it, Steve," Pitch said sympathetically. "We'll help more by leaving them alone."

Steve didn't say anything, but his eyes never left the doctor as the veterinarian's hands traveled down the right hind leg. In an attempt to relieve his anxiety he listened to the sounds from other animals housed somewhere in the building. He heard the incessant barking of a dog, the bleating of goats.

Pitch said, "He keeps only his small animals here. But he does a lot of work on the plantations for cattle, horses and mules. He's good. He's got so much business he needed someone to help him. Dr. Crane arrived a month ago."

Much later, Steve heard Dr. Mason tell his assistant, "It's a complete fracture of the proximal end of the tibia. We'll use a modified Thomas splint of light aluminum." Only the words *complete fracture* meant anything to Steve. He broke away from Pitch's grasp and ran to the table, fixing frightened eyes on Dr. Mason. "How bad is it, Doctor? Will he be all right?"

The doctor turned to him, annoyed at first, then tolerant and understanding. He put his hand on Steve's arm. "Don't you worry about him," he said. "Within three weeks that leg will be completely healed, and you'll forget he ever injured it. And so will he." Addressing Pitch, and motioning to him to get Steve out of the room, he said, "If you two will wait in my office, we'll get him fixed up all the sooner."

Pitch understood. He took Steve's arm and led him out of the room. Across the corridor was the doctor's office, and they went in there to sit down and wait for their colt.

8

The Giant

"WHAT time is it, Pitch?"

"One-thirty. It's only been a half-hour."

"It seems longer than that."

Pitch nodded. They sat in silence for another fifteen minutes. The boy rose from the couch, walked around the room, then sat down again, glancing at Pitch's wrist watch.

"We must remember to ask Dr. Mason about feeding the colt," Pitch said, hoping that conversation would relieve the boy's tension.

Steve nodded but said nothing.

"Unless we have to, let's not mention anything to him about Azul Island," Pitch went on. "The less people know about our being there the better. The colt's an orphaned foal; that's all we'll say. If I'm not mistaken the vet will just assume that we're keeping him right here on Antago. What else *could* he think?"

Again Steve nodded without saying anything.

The door opened and Dr. Mason appeared, his hand stroking his light beard. "The foal's ready to go," he said.

Steve was out of the office before Pitch had risen to his feet. He entered the large room across the corridor ahead of Dr. Mason. The colt was standing, his injured leg held in a fixed position by a crutchlike splint that began at his tiny hoof and ended in a large hoop around his rump. The veterinarian's assistant was with him.

Steve dropped down beside Dr. Crane. "He's all right?"

"Yes. He'll have no trouble. We've set the bone and the healing should be rapid." Dr. Crane's hands traveled up and down the light metal rods on either side of the foal's leg and then he examined again the heavy bandaging above and below the hock. "We've used plaster of Paris here," he explained. "There's no chance of his getting out of the splint. He'll be able to walk but not trot or run." His hand went to the hoop of the splint which encircled the colt's rump. "This is covered with soft leather, as you can see, so I don't think there'll be any chafing of the skin." Smiling, he turned to Steve. "You needn't worry about him. The bone's been set and now he just has to use a crutch for a while. It's as simple as that."

Dr. Mason joined them, his hands too checking

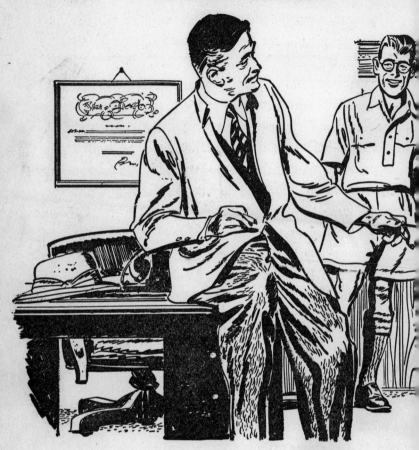

the heavily bandaged leg. "But keep him away from other horses, and watch his dam to make certain she doesn't push him around either."

Steve turned to him. "He doesn't have any . . ."

Pitch interrupted. "He's an orphaned foal," he told the doctor.

Dr. Mason rose to his feet, and Steve heard him ask Pitch, "You've been giving him cow's milk?"

Pitch nodded, and the doctor said, "He looks as though he's doing all right. How old is he?"

"Four days," Steve said.

Dr. Mason turned back to Pitch. "There's no reason why a foal, with proper care, can't be raised on cow's milk," he said. "It contains more fat and less sugar than mare's milk, but it's a good enough substitute."

"We've been adding sugar," Steve said.

Dr. Mason cast a searching glance at Steve, and then directed his next question to him. "How much milk have you been giving him?"

"About a quarter of a pint every hour except at night, when I give him a half-pint in three feedings."

The veterinarian nodded in approval. "There's more danger in overfeeding a young foal than underfeeding," he said. "A general rule to follow is to have him still hungry when he's had his allotted amount. I'm surprised you knew. A lot of people would have given him all he'd take at a feeding."

Pitch said, "Steve loves horses."

Dr. Crane spoke for the first time in a long while. "I can see that," he said, smiling at Dr. Mason.

"Oh, yes, and we wanted to ask you, Doctor, whether it's necessary to boil the milk and sterilize all the utensils." Pitch addressed Dr. Mason. "We've been doing that."

"It's very necessary for a while. You have to take the same precautions you would in the feeding of a human infant. Everything must be scrupulously clean, otherwise digestive disturbances are certain to follow."

Pitch glanced at Steve, then turned back to Dr.

Mason. "How long before he can be taught to drink from a pail?"

"Within a few days. You can start now by offering him the pail rather than the nipple and bottle. See if you can't get him to take it from the pail. The sooner you train him the easier it'll be for you."

Pitch saw no reason to tell him they hadn't been using nipples because none had been available on Azul Island. Just as he'd suspected, the doctor assumed they lived on Antago.

Dr. Mason turned to Steve. "It's safe now to increase gradually the amount of milk you give him," he said, "and lengthen the period between feedings until the foal is being fed only four times a day. I want to see him again in about twenty-one days. The bone should be completely healed by that time."

"He'll be all right until then?" Steve asked.

"I don't see why not. Just keep him isolated from other horses. I wouldn't want him kicked now. He'll get used to the splint almost immediately. He won't give you any trouble."

Pitch asked, "Would it be wiser to keep him here with you, Doctor?"

"No, there wouldn't be any point to it as long as you're able to keep your eye on him. And I'm out most of the day with Dr. Crane. I'd have no one here to care for him as you would."

"I want to take him with us," Steve said.

Pitch looked at him. "All right, Steve. I just thought it might be best for him under the circumstances."

Dr. Mason smiled. "Under the circumstances it's best that he go with you. Setting a bone is a simple matter compared to playing mother to a foal." Sympathetically he placed his hand on Steve's arm. "I want you to get a bottle of lime water at the drug store. Put four tablespoonfuls of it in every pint of milk you give him. He needs more calcium for a few weeks."

A little later they were back in the car, driving to town. The foal stood on the floor before the back seat, his head stretched toward the closed window. Steve sat on the seat, holding him steady, watching him, while Pitch drove slowly.

They were nearing the center of town when Pitch said, glancing into his rear-view mirror, "I keep thinking I see Tom's car."

Steve looked out the back window. "What kind of a car does he drive?"

"He's got a Ford, a maroon two-door sedan."

"There's nothing like that behind us."

"I know there isn't now," Pitch said, pulling up in front of Antago's largest drug store. "Just my nerves, I guess. I'm going to get the powdered milk and the nipples."

"And lime water," the boy reminded him.

While Steve waited he watched for a maroon Ford sedan. But he saw none and figured that Pitch had been mistaken in thinking he had seen Tom. Within a few minutes they'd be on their way back to Blue Valley where Tom never would find them.

Pitch returned, carrying a box containing the powdered milk, nursing bottles, nipples and several large bottles of lime water. When he had them in the car, Steve said, "The harness shop is just up the street. I want to get a web halter and a brush."

"Make it snappy, Steve," Pitch said, getting in the back of the car to hold the colt.

Steve was gone only a few minutes and when he returned with his packages, Pitch moved up front again behind the wheel.

"I don't suppose you'd consider boarding the colt somewhere on Antago," he said before starting the motor. "It might be wiser than taking him back . . . for his good, I mean."

Steve rubbed the foal's muzzle. "But where, Pitch? Do you know anyone we could trust, anyone who would take good care of him?"

"Frankly I don't, Steve. But we might be able to find someone."

"I wouldn't trust just anyone with him," Steve said thoughtfully. "If you knew of a good home for him it would be different. But I just won't take a chance. He'll be safe with us. We know that. No harm can come to him where we're going."

"I suppose you're right, Steve," Pitch said, starting the motor. "But he's going to keep you busy. You won't have much time for anything else."

They drove to the wharf. The freighter had finished unloading, but the activity on the wharf had not lessened for now Antago's exports, rum and molasses, were being taken to the waiting ship. Slowly Pitch steered the car through groups of perspiring stevedores, honking his horn constantly to avoid hitting anyone. They passed the long row of parked cars and trucks on their left without looking at them. They went to the far end of the wharf where they could park easily and leave the car until Pitch's next trip to Antago.

The foal hardly moved in their arms as they carried him from the car to the waiting motor launch.

Pitch said, "He's getting so used to being carried by us that the next thing we know he won't want to walk!"

Steve laughed, all his worry and tension gone. "I don't think so, Pitch. Someday he'll be as big and strong as Flame, then he'll be carrying us."

There was no longer any pain in the colt's eyes, only wonder and curiosity at everything Steve and Pitch did. As Dr. Mason had said, he was already getting used to the splint. He had no trouble standing, and Steve knew he would start walking the moment they gave him a chance.

"Well, we did everything we wanted to do," he told Pitch as the launch's motor burst into a roar. "And we needn't have worried about meeting Tom. My guess is that he did go to South America and it'll be a long, long time before you see him again."

"Yes," Pitch agreed, "you're probably right. We just caused ourselves needless worry. It wasn't even necessary for me to have given you the whole story on Tom."

"But I'm glad you did, Pitch. I'm in this as much as you are, you know."

Pitch headed the launch toward the open sea.

Neither he nor Steve looked back at the wharf, for now their eyes and thoughts were only for Azul Island. But if either *had* turned, he might have seen the Ford pull out of the line of parked cars on the wharf. It was a sedan, a two-door sedan, and its color was maroon.

Now it sped down the wharf, its motor racing, its horn blaring. The stevedores jumped out of the car's way, yelling; but when they saw the giant figure that dwarfed the wheel, they shut their mouths tight. They knew this man well. They wanted to have no trouble with Tom Pitcher.

He turned right when he came off the wharf, slowing down only because of a car directly ahead of him. He cursed, and his heavy hand never left the horn. He brought his front bumper hard against the car ahead. Startled, the driver looked back, saw Tom's face, and went faster.

Tom Pitcher went faster and faster as he tore through the outskirts of town and entered open country. Now his huge face showed no emotion at all; it held the deathly stillness and unnaturalness of a theatrical mask. A pallor showed beneath his tanned skin. His mouth was a thin, hard scratch of red, too small for the rest of him, as were his eyes. They were beady, snakelike . . . staring now at the road ahead without actually seeing it. He wore no hat and his black hair stood bristling straight, adding more inches to his giant's height. His white sleeveless shirt was open at the throat, disclosing his thick bull neck.

He turned down a dirt lane without slackening his speed. Fields of cane were on his left, the sea on his right. He glanced at the open water just once and momentarily his eyes came alive.

He drove on and on until he came to the driveway of a plantation. Turning into it, he passed the high barred corral, then the low, rambling house. He went on for another mile before bringing the car to a stop before steep, wooden steps that descended the cliff to the sea.

He sprang out of the car with a grace and swiftness one would not have expected from such a giant of a man. His feet, like his eyes and mouth, were small for the rest of him, and now they carried him softly, stealthily down the wooden steps even though there was no reason for quiet or secrecy. Yet he could not have walked any other way. Fondly, caressingly he touched the leather of the bull whip wrapped around his bulging waist.

Reaching the pier at the bottom of the steps, he turned once more to look at the point of land around which his stepbrother's boat must come. This time he saw it, and his short steps quickened as he made his way to his own launch, the *Sea Queen*.

Quickly he had her unmoored and the motor racing. He started out to sea, following the launch which was now less than a mile away. The chase had entered its final stage. He would follow his stepbrother, the boy and the foal to wherever they were going and then . . .

9

Black World

FOR more than three hours he stayed far behind the launch; it was only a tiny speck on the horizon. But this was enough for him to know they were headed for Azul Island. Until now the giant had not been certain that it was the destination of his stepbrother, the boy and the foal.

He had gone to Azul Island a few days ago expecting to find Phil's launch moored at the pier on the spit. When he hadn't seen it he'd known that his suspicions were correct . . . that Phil and the boy, Steve, had found something they were keeping very much to themselves. Deciding they never had gone to Azul Island, he'd combed the few islands to the west, looking for them. He had found nothing and so he had returned to Antago to wait, to pick up the trail again. And now he had it and them.

His long fingers, square at the tips, curled about the wheel. Where were they going on that island of yellow rock? Where else could they moor their launch but on the spit? Yet it hadn't been there before. *What had they found?*

His thin lids opened to disclose the greed in his eyes. He stared at the sun, already low in the sky. He wanted it to sink quickly into the depths of the western sea, for darkness was part of his plan.

He stared fixedly at the launch on the horizon. When night fell, Phil would use his running lights. But he, Tom Pitcher, wouldn't. He would trail, coming ever closer, following Phil and Steve to whatever they had found. He was no navigator but he knew beyond a doubt that Azul Island was their destination, for no other island lay in the direction they were taking.

He glanced up at the sun. There was at least another hour of daylight. His long legs, spread wide apart, trembled. Had he figured wrong? Would they reach Azul Island before dark? The speck ahead seemed even smaller now than it had just a few minutes ago. Were they outdistancing him? Should he go faster, pull ever closer to them even now? Take a chance on their seeing him?

He hated the sea! He was a hunter, more at home on land. He needed the earth beneath his feet, earth to provide tracks or a trail to lead him to what he sought. He increased the speed of the launch and the speck ahead grew larger.

The yellow dome of Azul Island appeared on the horizon. Desperately he sought more speed from the launch. But only a sudden sputtering came to him. And then the motor died beneath the sound of sea and wind. Frantic, he left the wheel of the wallowing launch to go below. Yet all he could do was to look at the motor without touching it. He knew nothing about mechanical things.

With angry eyes he stood before it, cursing the motor and the sea but never himself or his ignorance. Finally he thought of gasoline, remembering he had not filled the tank before his departure. Hurriedly he returned to the deck for the large can.

How long was it before he got the motor going again? Five minutes, ten minutes? He didn't know. All that mattered was that the launch he was following was out of sight, somewhere within the shadows of Azul Island.

His whole being was consumed with hatred for those who temporarily had evaded him. "Fools! Fools!" he said in a hissing whisper. "To think you can get away!"

Nearing the island, he placed a pair of binoculars to his eyes. He picked up the pier first and found no launch. Racing the motor, he turned away and spent the next hour encircling the island, studying the walled barriers against which the waves crashed. But he never ventured too close for fear of what the submerged rocks could do to the hull of his craft. Only when it became dusk did he take the launch to the pier on the spit. And now bewilderment filled the black pits of his eyes. *They were here, but where?* What had happened to their launch? It was too big to hide. Where were they?

He fastened his eyes on the mountainous rock rising above the spit. He looked at it a long while before turning away. Tonight he would sleep on the launch. Tomorrow the hunt would begin again. Somewhere they had left a trail, and he would surely find it.

Eagerness and anticipation absorbed his whole being now. After a while he went below, intending to eat, to satisfy the hunger that was already gnawing at his stomach. The chase on Antago had not given him time for lunch. But in the galley he found no food. In his excitement he hadn't thought of provisions either. Well, he would go without food tonight. But tomorrow would be different. Tomorrow he'd find Phil and the boy. They must have plenty of food, wherever they were. And what else did they have? *What else?* His thin lips drew back, disclosing his small, even teeth. His tongue ran along his lower lip as though tasting, savoring all the fine things that were in store for him.

The next morning he was up with the first gray light of dawn. His plan was to use the dory, which he towed behind the launch, to get as close as possible to the barrier walls of the island. With his binoculars he would be able to pick up any track Phil and Steve had left. He was certain that somewhere, somehow, Phil and the boy had penetrated the walls of Azul Island. Where else could they be?

He stood up and stared at the sea, then decided it was still too early to encircle the island in the dory. He was afraid of all small craft; the launch was bad enough, the dory worse. He might not be able to see the submerged rocks in the early light. He would have to be careful, too, not to be swept in against the walls by the waves. He didn't like any part of this phase of the hunt. Scaling the barrier wall from the spit would be much more to his liking. But could he do it? He'd never tried, but then he'd never had any reason before. There might be a way.

Taking two long ropes and a pick, he left the launch and walked down the pier to the spit. He stopped for a moment to tighten the bull whip wrapped securely about his waist, then he climbed to the top of the sand dunes. From there he could see almost all of the spit. Stretched before him was rolling land for a quarter of a mile before it met the sea on the other side. To his right the spit extended for a mile before disappearing into the sea. But he never looked in those directions. Turning to his left, he walked swiftly toward the mountainous rock that loomed less than a mile away.

He entered the canyon, his eyes squinting as he looked up at the sheer walls which rose on either side of him. He knew that his only chance of possibly finding a way into the interior of Azul Island lay at the end of the canyon. He remembered the ledge high on the cliff, which overlooked the spit. Behind and above it was a narrow cleavage in the wall which might mean something if he could ever reach the ledge to find out.

The small band of horses grazing at the end of the canyon ran when they saw him. But he paid no attention to them, for his eyes were on the end wall. The ledge, he figured, was about three hundred feet above the ground. His eyelids opened slightly as he scrutinized the wall beneath it. He considered the possibility of lassoing two protruding stones and reaching the ledge in stages. But the higher of the stones was still a hundred feet below the ledge. Still, once he was up there he might find something else above him to lasso. It was well worth a try.

He made his noose and coiled the rope. His long arm came back, then forward with the force of a giant spring. The noose of the rope settled around the first stone above and he drew it tight. He would have been surprised if he hadn't succeeded with his first throw. He tested his weight on the rope, then with the second coiled rope over his shoulder he pulled himself up, his feet braced against the wall.

Within a few minutes he had almost reached the stone. He stopped then to remove the second rope from his shoulder. Another seventy-five feet above him was the next stone to be lassoed. It was much smaller and he knew he was going to have trouble getting the rope around it.

Four times he failed, but with his fifth try the noose settled about the stone. Carefully he drew it tight, then considered his next step. Before removing the rope below him, he would go up the second rope to see if there was anything above which he might lasso that would get him to the ledge.

Gradually he put his weight on the rope above him. The noose slipped until there was only a small loop around the end of the stone. He knew then that it wouldn't bear his weight. He couldn't go up any higher than he was. Cursing, he lowered himself to the canyon floor and, leaving both ropes hanging on the wall, hurried back to the launch.

Perhaps later, if all else failed, he'd try the ropes again. But he knew there was little chance of his reaching the ledge, and his only alternative was to find the entrance which Phil and the boy had used.

Back at the launch, he put his binoculars in a shoulder bag and stepped into the dory. The small boat creaked with his weight. He hated going to sea in it, but there was nothing else he could do. The sun was up, the hunt was on! /

He rowed for more than a mile, his beady eyes shifting from the wall to the submerged rocks that seemed to lie waiting for him everywhere. Perspiration broke out on his large forehead, yet he continued rowing, continued looking toward the rugged shore for any trace or track of his quarry. He watched the sea beat mercilessly against the wall, sending its white spray many feet high in raging wrath at being stopped. Certainly Phil and the boy had never brought in their launch here! Perhaps farther on? But yesterday from his own launch everything had looked the same as this when he had encircled the island. Yet there had to be a way! Their launch could not disappear without a trace!

He kept rowing. Another mile, two miles? He didn't know. He stayed far enough away from the wall so as not to be carried in by the increased momentum of the swells as they plunged shoreward. Now his eyes were more on the submerged rocks about him than on the island. He knew he would have turned back long ago except that he dared not risk going back the same way. He had been lucky to get this far. He turned the dory away from the wall, seeking the safety of the outer sea. His face and body were wet with perspiration. He pulled hard upon the oars.

He heard the deep thud, the shattering of wood before he actually realized what had happened. Then the water began sweeping swiftly into the boat. He tried to plug the hole with his shoulder bag, but the bag was too small and he too slow. The boat settled quickly. He held on to its side until it disappeared beneath the surface, leaving him alone against the sea.

He swam toward the wall, fifty yards away. Strangely enough he was less afraid now than before.

He had feared the submerged rocks because he could not see them, because his tremendous strength could not be used against them. The waves which swept him closer and closer to the wall were an adversary he understood and could fight. Even if this was the end he was not afraid. There was nothing ignoble in dying this way, fighting.

The wall came ever closer and he swam hard to keep off the crest of wave after wave. He slid into deep troughs, plunging under water each time a wave would seek to pick him up and hurl him forward. His body scraped hard against the submerged rocks, but he felt no pain.

And then he saw the wall very close to him. One slip now and he'd be hurled against it. He plunged beneath a swell that curled upon him. When he came to the surface he saw the large moss-covered rock a few feet to his left. The white waters of the last wave were running down its sides, leaving it completely exposed. Furiously he swam to it and secured a hold as the next wave struck. The fury of the waters almost tore his grip away from the rock. But he held on to it as he'd never held on to anything before; then he pulled himself around the side of the rock to find still another rock behind it. Long and narrow and low, it extended to the wall.

He pulled himself onto it and lay there, breathing heavily. When his strength had returned he looked at the wall. He saw the thin ledge near the base. He noticed something else that caused his eyes to burn again with eagerness. The hunt wasn't over, as he'd thought!

When the next big wave receded, it exposed the low, narrow rock before him. Quickly he made his way to the wall, his hands clawing the rock, his feet slipping over its wet, green moss. Reaching the ledge, he turned to face the wall, his fingers groping for the piece of long thread that was imbedded within a jagged crack in the stone. He felt it between his thumb and forefinger. But he didn't look at it again. He didn't need to. He knew the thread was from Phil's bush jacket. And he knew from the feel of it that it had been there a long time, maybe a year. Perhaps when Phil and the boy had first come to Azul Island they had stood on this thin ledge with their backs hard against the wall, *the same as he did now!*

Turning to the right, he saw the shallow cleft in the rock at the end of the ledge.

Carefully he made his way to it and stood within the narrow confines of its three sides. The trail was as clear as if a note had been left for him. He saw the niches in the wall opposite him, one above the other for the full fifty feet of the cleft's height. He knew why the niches were there. He put a foot in one of them and braced his back against the wall behind him; then he started up, wedged between the sides of the cleft.

When he reached the top he saw the wide ledge, in the center of which was a stone shaft rising a few feet above the ground. He ran toward it, his face aflame. He saw the rope tied securely about the shaft and hanging down inside. Bending over, he looked down into the darkness.

"I've found you. I've found you!" he said in a whisper. Phil and Steve might be directly beneath him and he wanted to take them completely by surprise.

Putting a leg over the shaft, he tested the rope, then squeezed his body inside and started down.

He let the rope slide slowly through his hands while his feet scraped down the sides of the shaft. The light faded and he stopped a minute before descending any farther into the darkness. He regretted the loss of his flashlight which was in the shoulder bag he had so foolishly used in an attempt to plug the hole in the dory. He searched his wet pockets for a book of matches but found none. His hand caressed the leather of the bull whip still wrapped about his waist. At least he had that. Then he continued down the shaft.

Nothing would stop him now that he was so close to the end of the hunt! And perhaps it was better that he had no light. Phil and the boy couldn't be far away and he wanted to come upon them unnoticed. The light of the flash might have spoiled the surprise he had in store for them. His thin lips drew back as he tasted again the glorious fruits of a successful hunt. Who else but he could have found this trail? Now he had them! And whatever they had discovered belonged to him!

One hundred feet below, his feet touched the ground. He crouched, ready for anything. He knew he was in a tunnel and that what he had come down was a ventilation shaft. But he didn't stop to think, to wonder who might have built it or how long it had been there. It was enough that he was very close to his quarry; that was all that mattered.

The tunnel would take him to Phil and the boy; of that he was certain. They had traveled this tunnel and so would he, and it would lead him to them. Now he must be very quiet; he must steal upon them. He started down the tunnel, never hesitating before its blackness. The two he was seeking could be but a short distance away; it wouldn't take long to find them. Certainly the darkness of the tunnel wouldn't stop him now. He even increased his pace. He kept one hand close to the jagged wall on the right. That way he'd discover if any other tunnels diverged from this one. But he was certain he'd find none. Only one tunnel, he felt, could have been hollowed through this mass of yellow rock.

It never occurred to him that no human hands had cut this tunnel, that many ages ago a giant disturbance of nature had created it *and many others*.

He walked hunched over, bent almost double, to avoid striking his head against the jagged ceiling. It was a hard, uncomfortable position, but soon, he hoped, he'd be out of the tunnel. Soon he'd be leaving this blackness behind *to find them*.

He was surprised, even startled, to have the wall suddenly give way beneath his right hand. He stopped to grope, only to find another tunnel! He remained still in the darkness, trying to decide what to do. Finally he proceeded down the new tunnel. He would travel it for just a short distance and if he found nothing he would return and continue along the first tunnel. He felt no fear, only anger that this second tunnel had complicated matters for him. Now the hunt might take just a little longer than he'd thought.

How long he had walked he didn't know. It was difficult to account for time and distance in such darkness. He came to a stop, trying to pierce the blackness with his sharp eyes. He listened for sounds of Phil and the boy. But it was quiet, so quiet. And dark, so dark. His body trembled. He breathed deeply to still his trembling. But he didn't acknowledge the fear that was mounting within him. He went on and on.

Only when he decided that it would be best for him to return to the first tunnel was he aware of the warm blood on his hands. He must have been dragging them too hard against the walls, harder and closer than he'd thought. For a minute he rubbed his hands together, more in comfort than to ease any pain; then he started back.

At first he went at a slow, careful walk. A few minutes more, a few yards more, and he went faster; then he was in a run. As he straightened up a little too much, his head struck a jagged ceiling stone and he went down hard. He lay still for a moment, resting and seeking control of himself. He placed a hand on his head, felt the bump that was there. But it was not bleeding.

Getting to his feet, he began to walk very slowly. His hands felt another break in the wall, another tunnel. Could it be the first one, the one which led back to the shaft? He didn't remember passing any others. Should he go down it? Or should he ignore it and go on? His body started trembling again. And this time he accepted it for what it was, *fear*. Fear that he was lost! Fear of this blackness! Fear of the deathly quiet! And it turned suddenly to a savage hatred of the tunnels as though they were living, breathing things. He cursed them, cursed his step-brother and the boy and whatever they'd found. His voice rose shrilly in the tunnels and echoed back to him.

He started running again. He wanted only to reach the shaft that would take him to the light of day. He wanted only to escape, to see! But which tunnel would take him back? He went on and on, frantic and desperate. He came upon tunnel after tunnel. He turned down some, and passed others. He fell, got up and ran on. It was futile, never-ending. It went on hour after hour . . . perhaps even day after day. He didn't know; there was no way of knowing.

He was crazed with fear. He slowed his running footsteps, and groped feebly through the utter blackness. He fell again. This time . . . was it the hundredth or thousandth time? . . . he lay still for a long while, his face pressed hard against the cold rock. He stayed there until he felt the warmth of his own blood from his battered, cut face, then he struggled to his feet.

Hunched over, the weight of his large head and shoulders propelled him forward; his steps came rapidly as he fought to keep his balance. His dazed mind warned him he was going too fast for the many abrupt turns in the passageways, and he knew what would happen again. Yet he didn't care. Lurching, he wavered from one side wall to the other; then his outstretched hand struck solid rock in front of him. He tried to stop but couldn't. His body crashed hard against it, and he went down.

He couldn't have told later how long he stayed there. It could have been minutes or hours. Or even days.

When at last he opened his small, piglike eyes, they stared unseeingly for he made no attempt to penetrate the blackness all about him. He ran his tongue over his thin, cracked lips, but he could not moisten them. He was dying of thirst, dying of starvation.

His resentment against such an ignoble death for one who had risked his life countless times in physical combat brought forth a quick surge of renewed strength. His small, even teeth took hold of his lower lip as he raised his head from the floor of the tunnel and got to his knees.

He had slept; he was rested. His bleeding hands felt the wall in front of him. The passageway turned to the right here. He would follow it. But he would go slowly, conserving his strength. He was Tom Pitcher. He wasn't going to die *this way*. And no longer would he be afraid. Instead he would remain very calm.

Before rising to his feet, he ran his hands over his legs and body. No bones were broken. His skin was torn and bleeding from the jagged rocks, but that was all. He was all right except for his hunger and thirst. Well, there had been plenty of times in his life when he had gone for days without food and water. He could do it again.

He started to get up, his lips drawn in a bitter and hateful smile. Hadn't he found the entrance to the tunnels of Azul Island? But what lay beyond these tunnels? What had that weak-sister, Phil, and that kid, Steve Duncan, found that they thought they could keep to themselves? He'd find out. He was close to knowing.

When he was on his feet, weakness and then fright claimed him again. He shook his head to throw off this terrifying fear of the darkness, but his shaking only served to start his nose bleeding again. He put his hands to his face. And suddenly he was clawing his eyes and shouting. The sound of his voice, maniacal in its fury, reverberated up and down the never-ending tunnels.

"See! See! I want to see!"

Sometime later, he found himself on his hands and knees, crawling. He told himself that he wanted to crawl, that it was slower but less tiring. He began breathing faster, taking huge gulps of air. He thought that this would clear his dizziness. But it didn't. And again the fear of dying this slow, terrible death absorbed his mind and body. He crawled faster to get away.

Feebly he moved forward, thinking he was traveling rapidly yet barely moving. He thought of himself as still crawling when he lay quiet on the cold stone, his hands and legs outstretched. Convulsively his legs twitched in attempted motion, and for a long while his battered fingers moved. But finally the huge man lay still, buried thousands of feet beneath the surface of Azul Island.

Again, as for centuries past, the tunnels knew only silence. They were a world of their own, a maze, a catacomb of disaster for those who did not know them well. And Tom Pitcher was a stranger.

10

Early Training

IT WAS the third morning after their return to Blue Valley, and Steve knelt beside the foal, feeding him. He watched the quick movements of the colt's mouth as he sucked the milk through the nursing nipple. The large, bright eyes were on him, fearful that he would take the bottle away. Smiling, Steve turned to Flame, who stood behind them, watching and still curious about all that went on.

Steve talked to the stallion while feeding the foal. There had been slight indications at times that Flame might be a little jealous of all the attention the colt was getting. But never had Flame shown any outright animosity toward the colt. He was careful never to push him when he grazed near him during the day. And at night Steve always put the colt in Bottle Canyon.

Everything was going very well and Steve was thankful. Just as Dr. Mason had said, the foal didn't seem to mind having his injured leg held from hoof to rump in a fixed position. He went where he pleased at a slow walk, but Steve never let him stray too near the band. His early training had been started, too, for now he wore the soft web halter as if it always had been a part of him.

They were beneath the ledge, and Steve shifted his eyes from the stallion and the colt to where Pitch was sitting above. He saw his friend working on his manuscript. He was glad of that, too. Everything was as it should be again. Pitch was back enjoying the work he loved so much, while he, Steve, took care of the colt. Pitch left them pretty much alone now; perhaps he was still wary of Flame after his terrifying experience with the stallion when he'd tried to rope the bay mare.

The colt finished the milk in the bottle and held on to the nipple with tight lips as Steve attempted to take it away from him.

"That's enough. Nothing there but air, and that's not good for you to swallow." Steve pulled the bottle away, and rose to his feet.

Flame circled them, snorting, while the colt watched his sire. Steve snapped a lead shank to the halter. "Come on, fellow," he said. The foal, intent on following Flame's movements, hesitated a moment. Steve waited patiently until he had his attention again. For a few minutes each day he was teaching the colt to be led, to have complete confidence in whatever he asked him to do. His schooling now would make it easier later on, when the colt would be ever so much bigger and stronger and Steve *took him home*.

Finally the foal started forward and Steve walked a few more steps away. He went to the left, then to the right, the little colt following him. He stopped before the post to which Pitch had intended tying the bay mare. That post was useful to Steve during this early training, and now he tied the end of the rope shank about it and sat down, watching the foal.

The colt stood still a moment, then he drew back his head a little, feeling the tug of the rope. His eyes turned to Steve, and the boy talked to him.

If the colt had shown any sign of fear or fight, Steve would have released him immediately. But the colt accepted being tied. Steve went to him, unsnapping the shank from the halter and rubbing him gently on the muzzle.

Flame circled them again, his movements more spirited and restless. Watching him, Steve knew that the stallion was becoming impatient, that he had waited long enough for the attention he was seeking. Steve walked across the valley to the entrance of Bottle Canyon. Flame stayed right beside him; the colt watched them go, then followed at his slow walk.

Steve waited for the colt at the entrance to the canyon, then he put him inside and drew the long bars across. When he mounted Flame, the foal neighed shrilly. Steve felt sorry at leaving him behind but he had no alternative. He couldn't take a chance on the colt's following them again, neither could he spend all his time with him.

He felt the spirited restlessness leave Flame when he touched the stallion on the neck and leaned forward. Flame settled into his long, easy lope, but Steve felt the pulsating flow of power between his legs. There was no doubt that Flame wanted to go all out this morning. Steve knew what was coming.

From the lope, Flame went quickly into his gallop, each running stride greater than the one before. He held his head high, one ear turned back as though listening for Steve's slightest whisper of command. But none came. His ear pricked forward with the other, and he extended his head a little. The stallion knew he was being left to choose his own gate, his own speed. His tail spread like a red cloak behind him, and his mane suddenly whipped back.

Bending low, Steve pressed his hands and arms about Flame's neck. He had ceased trying to see ahead through his wind-blurred eyes, so now he closed them, conscious only of the terrifying speed at which the stallion was covering ground.

He rode and rode, and there was no slackening of stride. Beneath his hands he felt the rushing, heated blood of the great stallion. Was any horse in the world so fast as Flame? He opened his eyes, but still he could not see. He could only wait, wait for the stallion to run himself out as he wanted to do today. Perhaps he could have stopped him. Perhaps not. But he wasn't going to try. Flame would know when he'd had enough.

A long while later, the stallion's strides slowed. Steve sat back slightly then and with one hand wiped the wetness from his eyes. Apparently Flame had taken him to the far end of the valley and then turned, coming back. For now they were opposite the marsh and sweeping down again upon the band. Flame swerved to the left, then came to an abrupt stop before the band.

Steve saw no sign of restlessness among the band, so he slipped off Flame's back. He stood beside the stallion until Flame left him to join the band. Then Steve started down the valley. His heart was beating rapidly from the stimulation of the stallion's long run and the beauty and joy of being a part of this lost world.

When Steve reached the ledge, Pitch glanced up at him, said something that was garbled in his deep concentration, then turned back to the papers before him and continued writing. Steve went to the case of provisions, took out a can of pork and beans, and lit the kerosene stove.

"We'll have to get more food from the chamber,"

he said. "There are only a few cans left in this case."

Pitch never looked up, and Steve doubted that he'd even heard him. He got some biscuits and put those, too, on the stove to be toasted. Only when the meal was ready and he had put Pitch's plate before him did his friend stop working.

"Everything all right down there, Steve?"

"Very much all right," the boy said.

"How often are you feeding him now?"

"Five times a day."

"Good! And the vet said you could get him down to four."

Steve nodded.

"Are you offering him milk from the pail?" Pitch asked.

"Yes, but he prefers the nipple. I guess it'll take time to get him to drink from the pail."

"But keep trying. It'll make it easier for you. Does the milk still clog the nipple?"

"Once in a while. But I open it with the needle, as you suggested."

"Well, that's what Mrs. Reynolds did when milk clogged the nipples on her nursing bottles. I know. I watched her many a time." Pitch paused. Then, "But that's why I say getting the foal to drink out of a pail will make it easier for you. No fuss about that."

"I know, Pitch. I'll keep trying at every feeding."

"And his leg isn't giving him any trouble?"

"No. It's just as though he'd been born with that splint. He doesn't seem to pay any attention to it."

"Veterinary medicine has come a long way," Pitch said. "I remember the day when we couldn't do anything for a horse with a fractured leg but destroy him to relieve his suffering."

"And Dr. Mason said the leg would be completely healed in a short time," Steve said. "Just eighteen more days, Pitch," he added eagerly.

"Sure. He's young and bones heal quickly at his age. But it's different when it happens to old boys like me." Pitch laughed and rose to wash his plate in a bucket of hot water. "Not that I aim to let it happen," he added. "I'm a careful old codger."

Finished with his food, Steve stood up. "I guess we need another case of provisions from the chamber, Pitch. What we have here is pretty nearly gone."

"You said that before."

"I didn't think you heard me," Steve said.

"Sure I did. I hear everything. Even when you think I don't." Pitch glanced at the almost empty case. "We have enough to last another day or so. But maybe I'll go to the chamber later in the afternoon. I'm going inside anyway. There's another tunnel I'm following, Steve. I'm writing a description of it now, and I want to explore it a little more today, if I have the time."

A little later Pitch was once more back at his work, and Steve left to release the colt from Bottle Canyon. He didn't like leaving the colt alone or penned up except when necessary. After all, the colt had only him and Flame, and now the stallion was far up the valley, grazing with his band.

Pitch looked up from his writing when Steve reached the valley floor. He saw him going toward the barred entrance to Bottle Canyon and knew Steve would be spending the rest of the afternoon with the foal. He turned back to his work.

More than an hour later he had finished his writing for the day. He pressed his fingers softly but firmly against his eyeballs, seeking to rest them. Then he replaced his glasses and looked down at the valley. For a few minutes he watched Steve leading the colt on the rope shank, then shifted his gaze to the almost empty case of provisions. Well, he might as well get more food now. First he'd travel the new tunnel again, and on the return trip he'd stop at the chamber.

Taking his shoulder bag, he walked up the trail to the top of the waterfall where he stopped to take a long drink of the running water. He wasn't taking his canteen and this drink would have to last him until his return an hour from now, maybe two.

He entered the tunnel and followed the stream for only a short distance before turning into another passageway. He walked swiftly, his flashlight picking up the chalked figures and letters he had marked on the walls.

An hour later he arrived at the new tunnel. He went slowly now, discovering new chambers which he searched carefully for anything left behind by the Spaniards. He found another tarnished silver goblet, a sextant and a heavy spur with a sharp rowel. Finding these relics stimulated him in his search and exploration of the new tunnel. When finally he decided to go back he knew he must have spent much more time there than he'd planned and that outside it would be almost dark. Steve would be worried. He started back, going almost at a run, his light bobbing with the short, mincing strides he had to take in the low-ceilinged passageways.

He had almost reached the stream again when he thought of the food he was to have brought back. It would take only a short while longer to get it, and perhaps he wouldn't get a chance to go for the food tomorrow. He came to another fork and took a tunnel that he knew would lead him to the chamber.

He was almost there when he came to an abrupt, startled stop. The flashlight shook in his hand as its beam picked out the heavy body lying face downward on the cold stone. *Tom!*

Unable to move, Pitch stood there trembling. He

didn't know how long it was before he was able to make his legs move; then he went forward, slowly and as if stunned.

He found himself bending over the prone body. He turned it over, flashing the light on the bearded, scowling face. He looked upon it a long while before his numbed mind became active once more. He noticed the slight movement of the thin, dry lips. He felt the pulse and found it strong. He knew then there was nothing wrong with Tom that food and water wouldn't cure.

Still dazed, Pitch stumbled to his feet and left the giant behind. Blue Valley was but a short distance away. Food and water were there to save Tom's life. And *if* he brought them back, Tom would live to destroy Blue Valley.

II

Grave Decision

THE boy neither moved nor said a word while Pitch told him of Tom's presence in the tunnels. It was as though he had lost all feeling, all sense of everything, even fear. He seemed to be conscious only of Pitch's face, so taut, so ghastly in the yellowish glare of the lantern.

"If I'd found him dead," Pitch concluded, "it would have been better. I have no sympathy, no feeling for him any more, and he has none for me. I know he hates me for my shyness, my weakness . . . for being everything that he isn't." He paused to turn down the flame in the lamp. "Steve, are you all right?" He reached over toward the boy and shook him gently.

"I'm all right," Steve said finally. "It's just the shock, the . . ." He left his sentence unfinished.

Turning toward the stove, Pitch lifted from it a pot of heated soup and poured it into his canteen.

"I've got to feed him, Steve," he said. "I've no choice. We can't let him die."

"No, we can't let him die," the boy repeated in a voice that was barely above a whisper. He rose to his feet.

"You don't have to go with me," Pitch said. "He's unconscious."

"I want to go."

Pitch looked at Steve a long while before saying, "All right. Come along."

Steve kept close behind Pitch as they walked quickly through the tunnels. Gradually he recovered from the shock that had numbed his body and mind. Perhaps the fast walking did it. Perhaps it was Pitch's knowledge of this underground world, a knowledge that should be more than a match for Tom's brute strength. Whatever it was, Steve found a little warmth, a little hope in the darkness.

Because Tom had found the tunnels didn't mean that he had found Blue Valley, *that he ever would find Blue Valley!* Somehow, some way, they would keep him away from it!

But when Steve saw Tom's figure lying in the beam of Pitch's flashlight, he was again filled with fear of the man. He looked down at the giant, his terrified eyes widening at sight of the bull whip wrapped about the bulging waist. He wanted to tear it off, to hide or destroy it so it never could be used again.

"Help me with him," Pitch said. "Lift his head a little so I can get this soup in him."

Steve cupped the black, bushy head in the crook of his arm, while Pitch placed the canteen to Tom's mouth. The liquid wet the thin, cracked lips, and as it went down there was a quick, convulsive movement of the giant's jaw and throat muscles. Pitch poured a little more soup into Tom's mouth, then took away the canteen. "He's had enough for now, Steve."

They rested Tom's head back on the stone, and Pitch turned the light away from him. "We have no choice but to leave him here," he said grimly. "We can't carry him. If we could, I'd get him back to the spit before he regained consciousness. Sometime tonight we must decide what to do next." He flashed the beam on Steve's drawn face. "Let's go back. There's nothing more we can do *here*."

They had traveled a good distance when Steve remembered that he hadn't removed the bull whip from about Tom's waist. They were too far away to go back now; he'd do it tomorrow. But as he continued following Pitch he had a strange premonition that it was the one thing he should not have forgotten to do . . .

They reached their camp without having said a word to each other. The band had come down the valley, some of the horses grazing directly below while others drank from the pool. The colt stood not far away. But between him and the band was Flame, protective and ever watchful.

"You'd better put the foal in the canyon," Pitch said. "It's late for him to be out there."

Nodding in agreement, Steve fetched a bottle of milk and a nipple, both of which he had ready for the last feeding of the night. He warmed the milk while Pitch opened a can of hash for them to eat. Yet each was thinking only of Tom and what their next step should be.

After a few minutes Steve removed the bottle from the pan of hot water and shook a little of the milk from the nipple onto his wrist. It was still too cool for the colt. As he placed the bottle in the water again, he said, "Tom must have found the Chimney Entrance, the way we first got in."

"Yes, it's the only way he could have gotten into the tunnels."

Steve looked out over the valley. Flame was still there; the colt was safe from the band. His gaze swept to the cloudless night sky, and for a moment he seemed to be concentrating on the patterns the stars made. Then he said, "Pitch, when Tom regains consciousness he won't be *certain* we're the ones who fed him."

"Who else could it have been, Steve?"

The boy shrugged his shoulders. "But he'll be guessing. He can't be sure."

"He probably followed us. He knows we're here."

"If he had followed us, he'd know of the sea entrance," Steve protested. "And there was no one behind us when we came in. We both looked."

"I don't mean that he stayed close enough for us to see him," Pitch explained. "And since he didn't find our launch at the spit, he knew we were *inside*." He paused, then went on. "But let's assume you're right, Steve. What if he doesn't know for certain it's us? How would that help?"

"If we could blindfold him," the boy suggested quickly. "If we could just get him back to the spit without his knowing that it's us and how we got him out."

Pitch smiled grimly, shaking his head at the same time. "You don't honestly think for a moment we could do all that without letting him get his hands on us, do you? No, I'm afraid it would never work, Steve."

"Then what *can* we do, Pitch?" Steve asked desperately. "We've got to do something . . ."

"I know. I know, Steve. Maybe something will come to me. Go feed the colt."

Steve started for the trail, stopped, and turned to Pitch to say something. But he changed his mind when he saw Pitch's hands covering his face, and continued on down to the floor of the valley.

Flame came to him, neighing for attention. He straightened the stallion's mane and then walked toward the foal, Flame staying close to his side.

The colt had his forelegs bent, his small head lowered and just reaching the grass. He straightened at sight of Steve, stood quietly for a moment chewing the blades he held in his mouth, then spat them out and moved toward Steve.

The boy stretched out a hand and gently rubbed the furry body. He checked the hoop of the splint around the rump to make certain there was no chafing of the skin. The foal whinnied, reaching for the bottle in his hand. Steve pushed the soft muzzle away, and continued walking toward the canyon. The colt and Flame followed at his heels.

Steve fed the foal just within the entrance of the canyon while Flame stood by. The boy watched them both but thought only of Tom and what the giant would do if he ever found Flame and the colt and the band.

When the foal had finished, Steve put up the bars of the canyon. Flame nuzzled his shirt from behind. The colt neighed repeatedly from the other side of the gate, furious at being left behind. Steve lingered, waiting for him to calm down.

"Oh, Pitch," he pleaded aloud, "please think of something to keep Tom away. You know this world so well . . . you can keep him from ever finding them. He'll want the horses more than anything else here. He'll destroy them if he finds them. . . ."

Later, when he arrived back at the ledge, Pitch handed him his food. Steve took the plate but looked only at his friend's face. And he saw nothing that gave him any hope.

They said nothing while they ate. There were no sounds in this lost valley but the steady drone of the waterfall and an occasional nicker from a mare. Even the colt had settled down for the night.

"You haven't thought of anything, Pitch," Steve said finally.

It was a statement, not a question. But Pitch answered, "No."

They finished their food, then Pitch said, "I'm afraid our only chance is for me to make myself known to him, Steve. I'll remind him that he would be dead if I hadn't found him. I'll tell him that I'll take him safely back to his launch, if he gives me his word never to return or tell anyone what he's discovered."

"But he won't keep his word, Pitch. He'll be back if he doesn't turn on you before you get him out of the tunnels."

"What *else* can I do, Steve?" And when the boy

had no alternate plan to offer, Pitch continued, "I'll take him back the very same way he came in, then he won't know of Blue Valley."

"Unless he comes back later," Steve said. "And he'll do exactly that, Pitch. You know it as well as I do. He'll bring help, too . . . other men to help him find his way through the tunnels."

Pitch rose to his feet. "Yes, I know that. But it won't be easy for them to find Blue Valley. I can't think of anything else to do, Steve."

The boy's teeth were clamped hard on his lower lip, and he said nothing as he followed Pitch into the cave behind the ledge. At the far end Pitch stopped before the wooden box containing his collection of treasured relics. Lifting the lid, he placed inside the goblet and sextant and spur he had found that afternoon in the new tunnel.

Steve saw the cat-o'-nine-tails lying near the top and again thought of the bull whip which he had failed to remove from Tom's waist. Replacing the lid on the box, Pitch picked up the lantern and turned to him.

"This will sound very selfish to you, Steve," he said slowly. "But I'm taking this box to Antago early tomorrow morning."

"Why, Pitch?"

"Because, as you just mentioned, Tom could turn on me in the tunnels. He could force me to bring him here. For that reason these relics, my manuscript and photographs, everything that's of historical value must be kept away from him. I'm certain that Tom would wilfully destroy them if he ever got his hands on them."

"But the horses?" Steve asked bitterly. "What about them, Pitch? Don't you think they're as valuable as your . . ."

"They are. They are. I know, Steve." Pitch's words came fast in an attempt to stem the boy's anger. "But we can't possibly remove the horses from the island . . . except for the colt. You can take the colt."

Steve was still for a long while. When he spoke there was no anger in his voice, only hopelessness and despair. "Then you really think it's the end of everything, Pitch? There's nothing we can do to prevent it happening?"

"Not the end of everything, Steve. Perhaps the end of living here by ourselves, of going on with our work alone as we'd planned until we were ready to let the world know what we'd found. The wisest thing we can do, no, *the only thing*, is to remove what we can from here. And when we reach Antago tomorrow morning I'll place this box in the vault at the bank. No one will know what's inside. The president of the bank is a friend of mine and I'll leave with him a letter which he is to open only if I don't return to the bank within two days' time. The letter will explain how to reach Blue Valley."

"*If you don't return?*" Steve repeated, startled. "What do you mean, Pitch? Even if Tom does force you to bring him here, you'll be free to return to Antago."

"Will I?" Pitch's words were more for himself than for Steve. "I don't know what's going to happen." He raised his voice as his eyes met the boy's anxious gaze. "But the letter should bring help enough to stop Tom from destroying everything if I can't get back. And if the instructions aren't absolutely clear to my friends, you can lead them back. But I'd rather you didn't," he added soberly.

"*I lead them back?* Pitch! I'll be with you!"

"You won't, Steve. You'll go to Antago with me tomorrow morning and stay there."

"I won't. You'll need help if anything goes wrong. I'm coming back with you."

"You'll help more by leading our party back to Blue Valley if necessary," Pitch said, seeking to keep calm before the boy's defiance. "You'll be helping me and the band. You know as well as I do what'll happen to the horses if Tom ever has a free hand with them."

Steve looked at his friend for a long while but said

nothing. He didn't want to leave Pitch alone to face Tom. And yet, if anything did go wrong, he could lead friends back to Blue Valley just as Pitch had said. But wouldn't the letter serve the same purpose? The paneled doors above the sea hole could be left open, and those who followed would have no trouble finding it with Pitch's written directions. Meanwhile, he could be with Pitch to help him, if necessary.

Steve saw the hardness in Pitch's eyes, which told him as well as words that it would be useless to argue just now. A little later it might be different. But not now.

They returned to the ledge and stretched out on their blankets. Steve closed his eyes to induce sleep, which didn't come. His heart was beating very rapidly, as though he were doing some violent exercise. A frightening weakness absorbed his body. For the first time in his life his body shook with fear, and he sweated even though the night air was cool. He could think only of Tom and his bull whip; Tom in the tunnels, such a short distance away; *Tom in Blue Valley*. Was it the end, as Pitch thought?

He decided to get a drink of water. He told himself he was thirsty. But he wasn't. He wanted to stand, to walk, to rid himself of a terrifying weakness in mind and body. He went to the water canteen, only to find it empty. He welcomed the walk to the stream above to fill the canteen. He went up the trail to the great opening and gazed into its blackness, thinking of Tom. Then he turned away quickly to fill the canteen and to look out over Blue Valley.

It was a moonless night, but the stars were so close and there were so many of them that their light brightened the valley. Steve made out the dark silhouettes of the horses. He listened to them cropping the grass. He heard a short neigh from the colt in Bottle Canyon. He saw Flame moving quickly on light, ghostly hoofs across the valley. A few minutes later, the stallion had stopped to graze again.

Steve watched him, thinking of Flame's tearing teeth, his thrashing forehoofs and powerful, pounding hind legs. If ever Tom found Blue Valley, he would seek to dominate Flame. And the stallion would answer his challenge. It would be a terrible, horrible fight, one that never should be given the chance to start.

Steve descended the trail to the ledge. He put down the full canteen without taking a drink. But he felt better for his walk; the weakness had left his legs. Going to his blanket, he lay down again, hoping sleep would come. He needed all the rest he could get.

Tomorrow they had to face Tom, bargain with him. Pitch was right; there was no alternative but to go through with the plan he had suggested. They couldn't let Tom die. They couldn't keep him a prisoner within the tunnels. For if they did either, they would be as cruel and vicious as he. *They had to let him go*.

It was many hours later when Steve finally fell asleep, dreading the day to come.

12

Ambush!

PITCH, awakening a little before dawn, found that Steve was asleep. Good, he thought. He wouldn't disturb him.

Quietly he got to his feet. Steve did not stir as he heated the last can of soup and poured it into his canteen. Finally he turned away and started up the trail. His intention was to feed Tom now so he and Steve could get an early start for Antago. He'd return alone to Azul Island late this afternoon to bargain with Tom.

Entering the tunnels, Pitch turned on his flashlight. He didn't expect any trouble. He doubted that Tom would be conscious of what was going on. Soup was good for him now, and this afternoon when he got back he would give him something more substantial. With solid foods, Tom's recovery would be rapid. Tonight would be a good time to face him . . . before he got too strong again.

Pitch's steps quickened, taking him ever closer to

the giant whom he didn't know was conscious and already waiting for him.

Tom lay in the blackness of the tunnels, his eyes open and staring. He listened for the sound of footsteps, knowing that eventually they must come. He still retained the taste of chicken in his mouth, so he knew he had been fed. The renewed strength in his arms and legs told him so, too. He drew up a leg, then stretched it out again and drew up the other. He lifted his arms high, then brought them back to rest upon his massive chest. Again he listened for the slightest sound, but the tunnels were quiet. After a few minutes he sat up. His body wavered a little. Satisfied that he could sit upright he lay back once more and waited . . . *waited for Phil to bring him food.*

His thin lips were drawn back in what could have been a smile. Who else but Phil would have fed him? He closed his eyes to shut out the blackness of the tunnels which brought back all the agonizing memories of his fight for life. He hated this black, tomblike world. But soon, very soon, he'd leave it behind. He was alive. He'd won. Whatever lay beyond, whatever Phil and the kid had found was his! He'd play it smart. Perhaps Phil intended to leave him here to die. No, Phil wouldn't have the guts for that. He might intend keeping him a prisoner here but Phil wouldn't let him die.

"I'll just wait," he told himself. "I'll play along with him when he comes. I'll let him feed me again, thinking I'm still unconscious. And when he goes I'll follow him . . . *to find what he finds!*"

When he heard the soft footsteps on the stone, he opened his eyes. He smiled, for he would have known the sound of Phil's steps anywhere, any place, any time. For a moment he watched the bobbing light coming toward him, then shut his eyes once more.

His breathing was deep and regular when the light was directed on his face. He felt a hand lift his head; it was a small hand, soft and gentle, *Phil's hand*. The metal of the canteen was pressed to his mouth, and the soup was warm and good as it ran down his throat. He drank without opening his eyes. He waited. He wanted to smile again, but he knew it would only give him away and spoil his plan.

The canteen was taken from his mouth; his head was lowered to the floor. And then came the sound of Phil's retreating footsteps. He opened his eyes and sat up. For just a few seconds he watched the bobbing light, then he struggled to his feet. He swayed drunkenly at first, but the soup had given him additional strength and steadied him. Hunched over, he stole silently along the low tunnel, following the light that would take him out of this black world.

*   *   *   *   *

Steve awakened to the sound of a pan being placed on the stove. He saw that it was light and well after dawn.

Pitch said, "Breakfast is ready. I let you sleep."

The box containing Pitch's relics had been moved to the ledge. Seeing it, Steve remembered with startling suddenness and dread all that lay ahead of them on this day. He went to the stream to wash, and when he returned Pitch handed him his plate of bacon and toast.

"I've fed him," Pitch said quietly while Steve ate.

Startled, the boy looked up from his food. "You mean you've been to him already?"

"Early," Pitch said.

"Nothing happened?"

"No. He's still pretty weak, I guess. He didn't even open his eyes." Pitch finished his breakfast before speaking again. "The box will be heavy but I think we'll be able to manage it." Removing the lid, he neatly placed his briefcase, containing manuscript and photographs, on top; then he covered the box again.

Steve watched him without saying a word.

"I have a few personal things already in the bank vault," Pitch continued, "so another box of mine being put there shouldn't arouse anyone's suspicions. And it'll be nailed tight."

As he helped himself to more coffee, his hand

shook. He looked at Steve to see if the boy had noticed. Steve hadn't for his eyes were on his plate of
untouched food. "Eat your breakfast, Steve," Pitch
urged. "You'll need it."

Pitch said nothing more until the boy had finished
his food. "I've written the letter I spoke about," he
said. "So in case anything . . ."

"Pitch! Nothing's going to happen to you. Tom
wouldn't dare! He'll be only too glad that you'll
show him the way out of the tunnels. It's what will
happen later, when he's free and can return, that we
have to worry about."

"Perhaps. But I must be ready for anything,
Steve." Pitch paused, then intentionally changed the
subject. "You've decided to take the colt?"

Steve nodded.

"It's the wisest thing to do," Pitch agreed. "Until
we learn Tom's next move, the colt will be safer on
Antago. I'm ready to go, Steve. I'll help you feed
him."

"It isn't necessary, Pitch. I can feed him myself
just as I have been doing." Steve poured the last of
the milk formula from the gallon jug into the nursing
bottle. He wouldn't have to prepare any more until
he got to Antago.

"I'll go with you to feed him," Pitch said. "There's
nothing else for me to do. And the sooner we get the
foal fed and are on our way the better, Steve. We'll

take the box to the launch first, then come back for the colt. It'll be almost noon before we're ready to leave the island."

They went down the trail, Pitch hurriedly taking the lead. Reaching the valley floor, they started for Bottle Canyon. Steve saw the foal at the gate, awaiting him. In the distance Flame could be seen, grazing apart from the rest of the band. Steve knew his stallion would come to him when he and Pitch started up the valley, carrying the box. And Flame would follow them to the launch, unaware of the peril which he and they faced.

Steve lowered the top bar of the gate and stepped over the one beneath it. Pitch followed, replacing the top bar. "We won't let him out," the man said.

The colt eagerly reached for the bottle and Steve let him have it. Pitch's hands were on the silky body.

"He won't leave," Steve said. "You don't have to hold him unless you want to." He held the bottle higher, making it easier for the colt to get all the milk. "I probably could lead him at the same time we're carrying the box, Pitch. It would mean only one trip to the launch then."

"He might get away and hurt himself again," Pitch objected. "It's best if we make a special trip just for him. Besides, we'll have to carry him through the gorge. We couldn't handle him and the box too."

"Yes, Pitch, you're right."

They left the colt neighing repeatedly behind them and started across the valley again. Halfway to the trail, they heard running hoofs and turned to find Flame coming toward them. Pitch moved closer to Steve.

The red stallion reached them. He stopped abruptly, rose and pawed the air; then he whirled his giant body as though his hind legs were rooted to the ground, came down and bolted away. He cut a wide circle and came back, this time stopping in back of Steve to nuzzle the boy's shirt.

Steve ran his hands through Flame's mane, untangling the matted hairs; then suddenly he put his

arms around the long neck and pressed his head hard against it.

Pitch said softly, "Come on, Steve. It's getting late." He put a hand on the boy's arm, gently pulling him away from the stallion.

Flame followed them, pushing his body hard against Steve all the time. Only when they had reached the trail did he turn away and go back to his band.

Tears over which Steve had no control filled his eyes as he followed Pitch up the steep ascent. He stumbled on a small stone, regained his balance and went on, concentrating on the trail so as to avoid stumbling again. He didn't know Pitch had come to a sudden stop, and he crashed hard against him. He looked up. "Pitch, why are you . . ."

Pitch had one foot on the ledge. He stood there, not a muscle moving, deathly still.

And then Steve looked past him and saw Tom.

He stood towering above them, his pig-eyes burning brightly. The heavy whiskers about his mouth were dirty with food. He smiled, showing his small, square teeth. "Welcome back," he said. One hand reached out toward Pitch.

13

Snake Whip

EVERYTHING about Tom was as Steve remembered. He was hard, vicious, evil. Yet now he was helping Pitch onto the ledge. Such courtesy was foreign to this man. And when he spoke his voice was soft, too soft.

"It's good seeing you again, Phil." Tom turned his gaze on Steve, and the boy knew there was something different about his eyes, too. Hate and lust were still there, but mingled with them was a kind of terror, sadness . . . even *an appeal for help*.

"And you. Steve's your name, isn't it? Come up, Steve. Join us." He turned away and walked to the center of the ledge.

Steve was ready to run back down the trail, to flee from Tom at Pitch's first signal. But his friend's eyes never turned to him, never left Tom; yet Pitch said nothing to his stepbrother. Steve noticed the three empty cans, the last of their food, which Tom had finished. Pitch's briefcase had been removed from the box but was unopened; the rolled map lay beside it.

Tom was standing beside the box. Pitch moved forward, and Steve knew then they were not going to run away from Tom.

Pitch stopped a few feet away from Tom; he stood there silently watching his stepbrother. Finally he said, "Now that you know, Tom, I . . ." He stopped abruptly, for Tom had turned upon him.

Now, Steve noticed, Tom's eyes were the same as he'd remembered. No longer did they contain any sadness or fear or appeal for help. Only hate and contempt were there. Tom leaned forward, his body swaying a little . . . just his eyes seemed alive. But again he turned away from Pitch, this time to look out upon the valley. And when he spoke his voice was still soft.

"Now there's something," he said. He spoke as a man would speak if he owned the whole world. And he looked as such a man might look. "Imagine all this being here without anyone ever knowing." His eyes were following the movements of the band. Steve watched him, his heart sick, his body numb.

"Tom, since you now know we must . . ." Pitch's voice faltered again, then broke completely.

Steve turned to him, aware of the terrible fear that gripped Pitch. What could Pitch say that would matter now? They had to wait for Tom, to see what he would do. And now the giant turned to them once more, his little eyes staring. His lips moved but no words came, only sounds almost animal-like, choking and short.

Steve's heart was pounding hard, driving the numbness away. He realized now that they were not dealing with a sane man, that Tom was sick, *mentally sick*. Maybe Pitch had known it all along. Or maybe it had happened to Tom in the tunnels.

Tom's body stiffened. Like something inhuman, he uttered a growl, a snarl; then he was still. For a long time there was no change, then Steve saw the terror come to Tom's eyes again, the terrible sadness and fear and appeal for help. Yet there was nothing they could do for him . . . *or for themselves*.

He was walking now. He went to Pitch. "I finished all the food, Phil," he said, his voice still soft. "But you'll get more for me, won't you?"

Pitch nodded and turned away.

"Oh, not now. I've had enough for now. I wouldn't want you to leave." He smiled and only vengeance and hate were in his eyes.

"I found you," Pitch said brokenly. "You would have died, Tom."

Steve moved closer to his friend. Why was Pitch even trying to reason with Tom? It would do no good. They must try to escape!

"I know you'll get me food, Phil." Tom's voice rose until it became a contemptuous snarl; then he laughed loudly for the first time. "You'll do anything I want you to do, won't you? I can say kneel and you will kneel, crawl and you will crawl. I'm a little god, Phil, aren't I? I have power, absolute power. There's nothing I can't do *here*. And no one would ever know."

He turned toward Steve. "You, too," he said. "You'll do everything I say, won't you?"

Steve nodded without looking at him. He couldn't stand looking into those eyes any more. He wanted to run, but he and Pitch had to make the break together. Neither could be left behind to bear the crazed wrath of this man.

Tom stooped down. "What junk you have here, Phil," he said, removing the lid from the box. "What is it?"

"Relics . . . relics left by the Spaniards."

Steve saw the agony, the fear in Pitch's face. He supposed his own face looked no different. Tom was sick . . . he would kill if aroused or if he thought it necessary. But not now. He was going to take what he wanted, beat them down slowly, torturously, break them to his will. It was his way even now. He had not forgotten.

Yet knowing all this, Pitch was trying to be calm, to be rational with this man!

Tom straightened, holding a spur in his hand. "They knew how to make a horse mind," he said, fingering the sharp rowel.

Suddenly Steve felt the giant's blunt fingers on his shoulder. But they did not press deep into his flesh as he'd expected. Instead, Tom patted him. "Now, you're not at all like Phil," he said, and there was a mild friendliness to his tone. "You go after horses, not stuff like this. You got to that red stallion. I was watching you."

Steve's heart pounded and seemed to rise in his throat until he thought it would choke him. He never looked up at Tom.

The spur was cast to the ground, then Tom had the cat-o'-nine-tails in his hand. Fondly he fingered the whip with its nine hard leather cords.

"The Spaniards are getting more and more of my respect."

He snapped the whip, and one of the cords struck Pitch on the forehead. "So sorry, Phil," he said, smiling. "I'm not used to this thing."

Terrified, Steve watched the blood come from the cut on Pitch's face. But his friend didn't move, neither did he look at Tom. He stayed close beside the box, protecting its contents the only way he knew how.

"This whip isn't bad," the giant continued. "But it's for close work. You don't get any reach with it." Throwing down the cat-o'-nine-tails, he began removing the long bull whip from about his waist.

Steve felt his muscles contract. He saw Pitch's face get whiter still as the whip was unwound.

The long leather was now coiled like a snake at the feet of the giant. He held the short hard butt in his hand. "The beauty of the bull whip is that your opponent never gets a chance to get close to you," Tom said. "I'll show you what I mean."

They didn't need to be shown. They had seen Tom work his bull whip before. He knew they had.

Tom walked to the far side of the ledge, away from them and the box.

Oh, Pitch. Pitch. Let's run.

But Steve's words weren't uttered aloud. They, too, were within easy reach of the bull whip.

Tom didn't ask them to move. The bull whip was drawn back, its leather writhing venomously along the ground until Tom had it behind him. His big wrist and hand moved and a sharp crack came from behind him as though in warning of the blow to come. Then the leather moved over Tom's head so fast its movement was lost. There was another sharp crack as the end of the whip was flipped into the box, then silence. When Tom drew the whip out, he brought the sextant with it.

The leather was entwined about the sextant, and now it lay at Pitch's feet. As Pitch stooped down to pick it up, Tom flicked his wrist. The whip moved, and the sextant was released from the leather to be cast over the ledge. They heard it strike the cliff in two or three different places, then once more there was only silence.

The whip cracked again, this time picking up the spur which Tom had dropped earlier; it followed the sextant over the ledge. Then things happened so quickly that Steve lost all feeling, all sense of reality.

The bull whip beat a faster and faster rhythm until it became a weird chant. Steve never saw the grasping, tearing leather, only the effects it created. Half the relics in the box were cast over the ledge. And above the shrill screaming of the whip rose Tom's maniacal laughter.

Then suddenly there was quiet. Steve and Pitch stood white and shaking before Tom's inhuman rage.

"You were going to let me rot in there," he shouted at the top of his voice. "You thought you could . . ."

"He wasn't! He didn't!" Steve screamed. "He was going to take you out of the tunnels!"

The leather cracked at Pitch's feet. For a fraction of a second it stayed there, the pointed, fanglike end never moving. Without thinking of the consequences, Steve fell upon it, his fingers grabbing and tearing at the leather as though it were a living thing.

He felt it being pulled away from him; then Pitch was at his side, reaching for the leather.

They heard Tom's loud laughter as he came toward them. Fear swept through Steve, then a heavy
pounding filled his ears. He hurled himself at Tom.
Steve's right shoulder struck the giant above the
knees and with his arms he sought to pull Tom off
balance. The massive body swayed a little but Tom
didn't fall. Again came his laughter, and Steve felt
himself being picked up. Rough, angry hands placed

him on his feet, shook him, then sent him reeling backward. He was trying to regain his balance when he struck the wall behind him; his head snapped back against the stone, then all went black.

Pitch lunged at Tom even before Steve's limp body fell against the base of the wall. With all his strength, the small man struck out at Tom's face. He landed once, twice, then the terrible hands were on him and a massive fist struck him full in the face. He knew nothing more.

14

Escape

HOW long he had been unconscious, Pitch didn't know. He felt hands running over his body, probing, feeling and finally shaking him gently. He knew then that they didn't belong to Tom; Tom's hands didn't know gentleness. He tried to respond, to lift his head. But it felt much too big and heavy, and his efforts served only to blacken out everything again.

It could have been minutes or hours when once again he felt the hands. The pain in his head was less severe. He was able to make out the lantern burning against the wall. So he knew he was in the cave. Something big and blurred moved in front of the light. He stared at it a long time before he was able to make out Steve's face.

"Pitch. Pitch."

The boy's voice was but a whisper, yet Pitch heard him. He raised his head when he felt Steve's hands go behind him to give support. Then he sat up straight. Everything seemed to whirl crazily at first. He couldn't feel the weight of his glasses on the bridge of his nose. He moved a hand toward his eyes but Steve stopped him.

"You're going to be all right," the boy whispered, looking at his friend's swollen face. "Rest, Pitch. Just rest," he begged. "Don't talk now." He silenced the blackened lips with his fingers and moved closer to give Pitch more support.

Part of the ledge could be seen from where they sat, and Steve's eyes very seldom left it while he comforted Pitch. He knew Tom would be coming in again to find out if they had regained consciousness. For a long while it had gone on this way. Steve's head throbbed and he softly pressed the swelling on his crown to relieve the pain. But he knew his own injury was as nothing compared to the beating Pitch had suffered from Tom's fists.

The giant's figure appeared on the ledge and Steve lay back, pulling Pitch with him. "Be still, Pitch. He's coming." The boy moved away from his friend and flattened himself face downward on the stone.

Tom's heavy breathing and footsteps came ever closer until he was beside them. The giant stood there for many moments before turning away.

Steve waited until the footsteps told him Tom had returned to the ledge. Sitting up, he watched Tom scrape clean one of the empty cans of food. Tom wouldn't be coming back into the cave again for about another hour, he knew. Moving around the range of light, he went to Pitch. His friend sat up more easily this time and needed less help. "You feel better, Pitch?" Steve asked anxiously.

The man nodded and his lips sought Steve's ear. "How long?"

"About three hours," Steve told him. "It's almost noon, judging from the light outside."

Pitch looked in the direction of the ledge and the glazed, stony expression left his eyes when he saw Tom. He watched him for a long while without saying anything.

"He's waiting for us to regain consciousness," Steve said.

Pitch turned to the boy and his gaze found the large swelling on Steve's head. But he said nothing before turning back to watch Tom. Finally he drew his legs back and forth, working them, and then he moved his arms. "In a little while now, Steve," he whispered. "A little while, and I'll be ready."

Steve knew Pitch meant they were going to attempt to escape.

An hour passed, then they saw Tom start toward them again. They stretched out, their faces pressed hard against the stone floor.

Steve heard Tom come, then felt his heavy presence. The light of the lantern was turned on him and one of Tom's big hands lifted his wrist, feeling his pulse. Then the giant went to Pitch. Steve guessed he was turning him over, for Pitch grunted. There came the splash of water against Pitch's face, followed shortly by the sharp clang of the empty canteen as Tom let it fall to the floor. Pitch only moaned and did not stir; his heavy breathing filled the cave.

Tom made no further attempts to revive Pitch; it was as though he knew he had plenty of time and could afford to wait. He turned away and left them alone again.

Pitch sat up before Steve did; he moved out of the range of light and rose unsteadily to his feet. "Get up, Steve."

They stood behind the light, moving slowly in place to relieve their cramped muscles. Yet all the time they watched Tom as he sat on the ledge and looked out over the valley. Steve felt sure that what held Tom's attention were Flame and the band.

A short time later they saw Tom get to his feet and start down the trail to the valley. Pitch placed a hand on the boy's shoulder, and his pressing fingers told Steve this was their chance to escape from the cave and Tom.

"*Now*," Pitch said. He went to the lantern and, grabbing it, extinguished the light. "Come on!"

They moved quickly through the cave, but stopped when they reached the ledge. It was littered with pages of Pitch's manuscript; the chest was turned upside down and the relics which had not been cast below were strewn about. Tom was on his way down the trail.

Pitch stumbled as he pushed Steve in the direction of the upward trail. "Get going," he said. "I'll follow."

Steve started up, then stopped and turned around. Pitch wasn't following him; *he was picking up the pages of his scattered manuscript!*

Steve had started back to help him when he looked down the trail and saw Tom turning back in their direction. "Pitch!" he shouted. There was no longer any need to keep his voice low.

Pitch paid no attention to Steve's cry of warning except to pick up the pages faster, clutching them to his chest. Running to him, Steve pulled him away as Pitch recovered the last of the pages. A swift backward glance told Steve that Tom was coming up the trail. Steve knew he could reach the tunnels above before Tom did. But could Pitch?

They ran across the ledge to the upward trail, and Steve pushed Pitch ahead of him. Then, stooping, he picked up the cat-o'-nine-tails as he went across the ledge to meet the giant. He had to hold Tom back long enough to give Pitch the start he needed.

Steve reached the trail when Tom was but a few feet below. He swung the whip, bringing its lashes hard against the giant's chest. Bellowing in pain and rage, Tom threw himself backward and for a moment lay on the trail, looking up at the boy. Tom's piglike eyes were red with fury as he pulled himself back along the trail out of range of the whip; then he got to his feet and quickly began unwinding the bull whip from about his waist.

Steve waited, knowing the cat-o'-nine-tails was useless against the long bull whip. He had done all he could, but every second he kept Tom here meant a better chance for Pitch to get away. He took one quick look up the trail and saw that Pitch was still climbing, apparently unaware that his friend wasn't right behind him. Another few seconds and Pitch would have reached the tunnels.

Suddenly the crack of the bull whip burst in Steve's ears and he fell backwards as the leather cut into his chest. He managed to regain his feet before striking the ledge, and his outstretched hands broke the force of his fall. Then he moved with the swiftness of a sprinter. He kept low, his body crouched, his running steps coming fast and short. The whip cracked above his head, but it only served to urge him to greater speed.

Reaching the trail, he started up without checking his fast pace. He watched for stones, well knowing what a fall would mean. He took his eyes off the trail only once. Above he saw Pitch stopping at the entrance to the tunnels. "Go on!" he shouted to him.

Tom was so close on his heels that Steve could hear

his heavy breathing, and his strides quickened even more. But suddenly a sharp cry came from behind. Steve didn't have to look back to know what had happened. Tom had fallen! Here was another chance to gain valuable distance! It wasn't until he had reached the entrance to the tunnels that he heard Tom's footsteps on the trail again.

Now he looked into the great opening for Pitch. There he was, traveling the right side of the underground stream. Steve followed him, catching up with him as he was going around the bend of the stream. Dead blackness lay ahead. Pitch told him to put his hand on the back of his belt; then they went on without once looking back.

They stopped at what Steve knew must have been the first fork in the tunnels, for he could find no wall to touch with his right hand. Pitch was breathing heavily, and he made no attempt to go farther.

Something rattled in Pitch's hand. Steve guessed it must be a box of matches, but Pitch did not strike a light. When he spoke, he sounded tired. "We'll wait a few moments, Steve. I don't think he'll have the nerve to follow us, but we must know for certain."

They stood there, watching for a light that would mean Tom had entered the tunnels. There would have to be a light for Tom would never enter the tunnels without one. And even with the lantern or

flashlight would he have the courage to face this underground world again? Steve doubted it, as did Pitch, and the minutes passed with no evidence that they were wrong.

Then, suddenly, the yellowish glare of the lantern broke the blackness. It came around the bend of the stream and toward them. Slowly it moved, then slower still until it came to a stop. Pitch was gripping Steve's arm; both were ready to run again.

But the light came no closer. Instead Tom screamed angrily at them. They were hysterical and meaningless words, which echoed and re-echoed, then finally died within the tunnels. A few minutes later the light retreated until it could no longer be seen.

"Come, Steve."

Again the boy took hold of Pitch's belt, going with him down the right fork. They spoke no more in the blackness and stopped only occasionally when Pitch lit a match to look at the chalked figures and letters on the walls of the tunnels. Within a short while they entered the large chamber where the extra supplies were stored.

Pitch lit a lantern, then leaned heavily against the table. "We'll rest . . . that's all we can do now."

"Tom is mad, Pitch. No man in his right mind would act as he did."

"Sick," Pitch corrected in a hoarse whisper. "He's sick mentally, Steve."

"Did you know? Have you known all the time?"

Pitch shook his head. "No. He's been harder to get along with the last few months, as I told you. But I took it for restlessness. I never suspected . . ." His sunken eyes rose to meet the boy's. "Perhaps his ordeal in the tunnels did it, Steve. I don't know. But the tunnels could have done it to him. We've got to get away. We must get help . . . a doctor . . . somebody. It's our only chance . . . *his only chance ever to get well."*

Neither spoke for a long while. The yellow light bared the room and their fear. They still had not reached the launch. And it was their only means of getting help.

"Is there no way to get from here to Blue Valley without . . ."

"Without going down the trail again and past Tom?" Pitch finished for him. "No, Steve, there isn't. It's the only way."

15

Red Sentinel

A HALF-hour later, Steve walked dazedly about the chamber. He stared at the Spanish coat of arms cut in the wall behind the table, but he didn't actually see it any more than he saw the blue sky when he gazed up the ventilation shaft that penetrated the hundreds of feet of rock above the chamber.

He was thankful for the food he had just eaten, thankful to Pitch for having had the foresight to keep supplies here for use in an emergency. For this was indeed an emergency. It was true that for the time being they were safe from Tom; there would be no more beatings, no more pain *providing* they were careful. Yet they were still his prisoners. There was no way to reach the launch except through Blue Valley. No way to reach Blue Valley except to go back the way they had come.

Would they be able to get past Tom during the night, as Pitch planned? Even if they watched and slept in shifts would the moment come when Tom would be sleeping so soundly that they could get by the ledge in safety? They would be taking a terrible chance, but what was their alternative?

And even if they were successful, where would it all end? What would Tom do while they were gone for help? What would happen to Flame and his band? And to the colt? Would Tom touch him, hurt him? The colt would be frantic with hunger; he might even do himself harm. But, as Pitch had said, the colt could go a day, perhaps two days, without food . . . and by that time they'd be back with help.

It was Flame's safety that would worry him more than anything else even if they did get away. Tom's hard hands were skilled in breaking horses in the only way he knew how. And Steve knew the slightest spark could touch off a horrible battle between Tom and Flame. It could happen any hour, any minute . . . *even now.*

"Oh, Steve. Steve."

It was Pitch, and his words carried all the pity and suffering and sadness of a man in pain too great to bear. His face was buried in his hands as he sat in the chair behind the table.

Steve stood still, just looking. He was afraid to move, to speak. He waited, his fearful eyes on the bent head before him.

Finally Pitch spoke again, but his hands still covered his face so that his words were just mutterings.

But Steve made out one word and it was enough to make him freeze still more.

The map!

Tom had it! When they had fled, Pitch had taken his manuscript but they had left the map behind. On the map was marked the way to the launch. Tom could leave the island now, leave them to die here if he wished! And then he could return in his own time to do as he wanted with this lost world.

Pitch was the first to move. He staggered to his feet and started across the chamber. "We must go back," he said hoarsely. "Now."

When they reached the bend of the stream, they got to their hands and knees. They crawled a few feet at a time, stopped, listened and went on. Just within the great opening they flattened themselves down even more, twisting and squirming over the cold stone.

Slow now, and listen. Listen for any sound of his footsteps on the trail. He may be there. He could be just outside the opening, waiting and ready. Keep close to the stone. But be set to run back if he's here, if he sees us. Don't talk. Don't breathe. We're almost in the sunlight. We can see the top of the trail and he isn't there, waiting as he might have been. A few more feet and we'll be in the sunlight. We'll be able to look down at the ledge. But listen first. Listen for any sound of footsteps. Could we hear him above the drone of the falls? Yes, yes we could. Go forward then, but keep flat. We're outside. We should be able to see him now. Or has he already gone to the launch? Take a deep breath, hold it and look for Tom!

Their eyes swept down the trail to the ledge. Tom sat on a wooden box, the map spread before him. Then they still had time! But for what? How could they prevent Tom from reaching the launch? Jump him? Fight him? *No! No!* What chance did they have to stop him? They could only watch and wait and hope.

Tom got to his feet and stood looking toward the marsh. The way to the launch would be easy for him; he had only to follow the map Pitch had drawn so well in detail. But he wasn't going yet; instead he opened the can of whole milk and, mixing powder with water, swallowed it in long gulps.

They watched him, aware that the milk appeased his enormous appetite but did not by any means satisfy it. Soon Tom would go to the launch in the hope of finding food there. When he found none he would go on to Antago. He would return with provisions immediately or he would wait for them to die of starvation before he returned. They had enough food in the chamber to last them a week, perhaps a little longer.

Steve heard a short, shrill neigh from the colt in

Bottle Canyon. It was time for his feeding; he was becoming impatient. Was this then the end for him, too?

Pitch whispered, "Our only chance is that Tom doesn't go to the launch today, that we can get past him during the night."

The band had come down the valley. The mares with suckling foals were closest; some of them went to the pool while others grazed near the cane. Yearlings and weanlings were scattered, grazing and playing in small, separate groups. Flame had come down with them but had gone directly to the barred gate of Bottle Canyon. He stood there, listening to the incessant neighing of the colt on the other side.

Steve watched Flame and so did Tom. Finally the giant turned, looked in the direction of the marsh again, then at the map. He studied it for a little longer before rolling it up.

Pitch and Steve could tell that Tom was trying to make up his mind whether to go to Antago that day. It was past mid-afternoon. If he left then it would be dark before he reached Antago. It would mean a night voyage. Tom was no navigator, no seaman. He wouldn't like being on the open sea at night. But his hunger might compel him. . . .

They saw the bird rise from the cane, startling a few of the foals and causing them to move hurriedly back to their dams. Tom had seen the bird, too, for now he put down the map and his hands moved to the bull whip about his waist. When he started down the trail Steve and Pitch knew he was going after the bird.

They waited until he had reached the valley floor, then they hurried down the trail to the ledge. Pitch looked at the relics strewn about, but he picked up only the rolled map.

Then he and Steve fell flat on their stomachs again. They didn't want to be seen by Tom or by Flame. The stallion would betray their presence on the ledge if he saw them. He had moved away from Bottle Canyon, then had come to a stop, watching Tom. But his eyes, his movements disclosed only curiosity and interest in the man who was walking slowly toward the pool. He had no reason not to accept Tom.

If Tom had seen the stallion, he paid no attention to him. He walked past Pitch's snubbing post, intent only on the place in the cane field where the bird had come to rest. The mares moved quickly away at Tom's approach. The bronze shoe stirrup lay gleaming on the ground where it had been cast from the ledge; near it were the silver goblet and horseshoe; a little beyond were the long lance, the helmet, and the sextant.

Tom went around the pool to the edge of the cane. His bull whip was ready. His wrist was bent back, the long leather whip trailing behind, straight and still now. But any second it would strike, its movement so fast it would be lost to the eye.

Steve and Pitch could only wait and watch. Tom was still between them and the marsh. They remained his prisoners. A mare whinnied, breaking the ominous stillness. It was the bay mare, but the twin filly was not beside her. The mare had turned toward the cane, her eyes startled, worried. She whinnied again.

Deep within the cane, Steve saw the little filly's head. She answered her mother's call, then the cane stalks bent as she started for the mare. Her movements were frantic for she was small and the cane high. She neighed repeatedly and sought to keep her head above the stalks as she neared the cropped grass of the valley floor and Tom.

The nesting bird was flushed by the filly's movements and neighs. With its rise in the air came the crack of Tom's whip. There followed the flutter of flying feathers. But the bird escaped! Tom's head moved simultaneously with its flight, and Steve and Pitch could sense the anger and fury that burned within him at his near miss. Another second, another foot closer and his hunt for food would have been successful.

The filly had come to an abrupt stop at the crack of the whip. She stood still for a moment, trembling

and uncertain. The mare neighed shrilly, and the filly turned to go to her.

But she moved too late. The crack of the whip came again and with it Tom's enraged bellow. The leather bit into the filly's slender haunches. Squealing and terrified, she bolted. Tom ran crazily after her, chasing her around the pool and almost back to the mare.

Every horse in the band was moving now, scattering, neighing, running. But their hoofbeats were deadened beneath Flame's whistle. Tom turned toward him, as did Steve and Pitch. They saw Flame galloping across the valley to attack Tom. Steve's fingers found Pitch; he pressed hard, realizing that what he had feared most of all was about to happen.

Tom did not run. He even turned his face away from the stallion, the better to gauge the distance to the trail. It was less than thirty feet. He could reach the trail easily if he ran. But he didn't run. He had never run from a horse, from any animal, in his life. He was not afraid. Instead he was more elated, more excited than he'd been in a long, long time.

Close to the trail he stopped and turned to meet the oncoming stallion. The long leather of the bull whip was behind him; his wrist was drawn back and ready. He saw the fire in the large, lustrous eyes of the horse. And his own eyes gleamed with a light equally bright. He moved his feet wider apart and his eyes narrowed until they were mere slits. He saw the red stallion gather himself for the quick, sudden stop and attack to come. His wrist tightened and his fingers pressed hard into the leather of the whip's handle.

With bared teeth the stallion came to an abrupt stop fifteen feet away from him, just as Tom had known he would do. Tom watched as the stallion snorted and rose on hind legs to his full height. Then Tom stepped back quickly; his whip cracked, its biting end tearing into the stallion's belly. Screaming in pain, the horse came down. Again Tom struck and the bull whip tore into Flame's neck and withers.

Tom's face was distorted in evil rapture. Here was a horse who would give him a fight worthy of his great strength and skill! He was pulling back the long leather he so foolishly had let encircle the stallion's neck when the horse suddenly jerked his head, tearing the whip from his hands. He started forward to retrieve it but was too late.

Terrible in his rage, the red stallion rose above him. And for the first time in his life Tom knew what it was to fear an animal. Certain death was coming down upon him. He hurled himself away from the thrashing forelegs, feeling one graze his shoulder as he fell to the ground. Quickly he rolled again and again, and then he felt the stone of the trail beneath his frantic hands. His face white and terrified, he scrambled upward, expecting to feel the terrible hoofs crushing his back. Only when he was well up the trail did he realize that the path was too narrow and steep for the stallion to follow and that he was safe. Turning around, he saw Flame pounding the long leather of the bull whip.

Slowly Tom regained his composure. "I'll break you yet, you stud horse!" he shouted hysterically, repeating the words over and over as he sat watching the stallion in all his terrible but, to him, beautiful fury. His hunger for the time being was completely forgotten as he made his plans to beat this horse that knew no master.

16

Challenged!

STEVE and Pitch left the ledge as soon as Tom started up the trail. He hadn't seen them for he was too frantic then to have noticed anything. Now they stood just within the great opening of the falls again, breathing heavily from their fast climb.

"Flame almost killed him, Pitch. *It would have been all over.*"

Pitch looked at the boy's white face a long while before saying, "We can't think that way, Steve. He's sick. We must think only of getting help."

"But he'd kill us, Pitch. I know he would."

Pitch had nothing more to say.

Once more they got down flat on their stomachs and crawled toward the sunlight. They had to watch Tom, to make certain he wasn't coming up the trail. Pitch made Steve stay behind him; it was only necessary for one of them to act as lookout.

Now Pitch could peek down. Tom was standing on the ledge, watching every move made by the red stallion. From time to time he shouted at Flame. Finally, when Flame moved away to return to his band, Tom searched the ledge for the rolled map. When he could not find it, he looked up in the direction of the trail.

Pitch flattened himself still more against the stone. He didn't think Tom could see him, but he couldn't be sure. There was no need to raise his eyes; his ears would tell him of Tom's approach. And at the slightest sound of a step on the trail, he and Steve would start running.

But no footsteps came, only Tom's voice. And his words were all the more startling because of the softness with which they were uttered.

"I know you're up there, Phil," he said. "But I'm not running after you any more. I don't need to. You're going to come to me."

Pitch felt Steve's clawing hands on his legs, attempting to pull him back.

Run! He'll be coming. He knows we're here!

But still there were no footsteps on the trail. Instead Tom's voice came again.

"We'll talk this over, you and me, Phil. You're there. I know you're there."

Steve pulled Pitch back within the opening. "Don't believe him, Pitch. He won't talk it over. He'll . . ."

Tom's voice came once more, still calm, but now the softness was mingled with his hatred for them.

"I don't need the map any more to find your launch," he said.

They hardly heard his words; they were listening only for his footsteps on the trail.

"You'd better come down, Phil. You'll have to, anyway. You can't reach your launch without coming down here. I know that, otherwise you'd be gone by now. Phil, are you listening? Do you realize what's going to happen? What I can do? You know very well, don't you, Phil?"

His laughter reached them now, low at first, almost a cackle, then rising until it was hideous in all its madness. Then, "I'm not going to ask you again, Phil, so you'd better come down."

For a long while, there was only the drone of the waterfall. No words, no footsteps. Their bodies sweated and ached with their tenseness; their legs were ready to carry them back into the blackness where Tom never would follow them.

Then his voice came again. "You've had your chance, Phil. You should have known better than not to come to me. I'm going to let you rot here. I'm taking your launch tomorrow morning. I'm going home. And do you know what, Phil? I'm not coming back for a long, long time, not until you're dead. Not until you starve *as you were going to let me starve.* . . .

"It's too late now, Phil, but you should have thought of the kid. He's pretty young to die. And it'll be your fault, Phil. You should have thought of him."

Pitch made no move but his face was ghastly white.

"Don't listen to him," Steve said desperately. "We know he wouldn't give us a chance. Tonight, Pitch . . . tonight we'll get past him."

Pitch said nothing, and there were no further words from Tom.

They stayed there, knowing Tom couldn't be certain that they were here, for he hadn't seen them. They would not go back to the chamber; it was best that they remain here, watching, waiting for the slightest chance to get past Tom before morning.

From time to time during the late afternoon, they crawled out of the great opening to look down upon the ledge. They saw Tom descend the trail to the valley floor to retrieve his bull whip. The remainder of the day he spent watching Flame's movements with the band. He saw the great stallion come down the valley often in answer to the incessant neighing of the colt in Bottle Canyon. Tom must have recognized the colt, for he looked at him for a long time after Flame had returned to his band. Once he started down the trail as though to go to the canyon gate, but he stopped when Flame came down the valley again. Back at the ledge once more, Tom sat down, his thoughtful gaze leaving the stallion only for the snubbing post below.

Shadows fell quickly and heavily over the valley with the sinking of the sun behind the walls. Night would soon follow, and with it would come Steve's and Pitch's only chance of escape.

Pitch spoke to Steve, still keeping the side of his face pressed hard against the stone.

"He'll have to sleep sometime," he whispered. "I'll keep the first watch and call you when I feel I'm getting drowsy, then you take over."

"I'm not sleepy," Steve said. "I don't think I will be."

"In a few hours you will."

Somber blackness came to the valley. Even the stars seemed fewer and farther away that night as though they too would do all they could to conceal Steve and Pitch from Tom. But the yellow light of the lantern gleamed below, exposing the ledge as bright as day.

They watched Tom pick up all the empty cans and scrape them clean into a pot of water he had on the stove. Finally he lifted it to his lips, drank from it in great gulps, then hurled the pot against the stone. He strode about the ledge, every stride giving evidence of his fury and hunger. He looked up in the direction of the trail, but there was no chance of his seeing Pitch and Steve in the darkness.

The colt had been neighing constantly, yet there was nothing Steve could do for him. Or that Flame could do. The stallion made frequent trips down the valley to the barred gate of the canyon, but his visits only brought forth more and louder outbursts of frenzy from the colt. Steve could not see Flame in the darkness but the beat of hoofs told him when the stallion was at the gate and when he left to return to his band.

"Flame could keep Tom from going up the valley and reaching the launch," Steve said grimly.

"I doubt it. Tom has handled wild horses like Flame before. He has his ways. No, our only chance is to get by him tonight. Try to go to sleep now, Steve. It's getting on."

The hours passed, but it was impossible for the boy to sleep. Always there was the light below, and beyond in the darkness the frantic appeals from the colt. How could he sleep? How could anyone sleep tonight? *Even Tom.* They could only pray and wait and hope that he would.

More hours of waiting passed with never a closing of an eye for either Steve or Pitch. Was it early morning yet? It must be, for even the colt was still now and there was no sound from Flame or the band. Yet below the light was still burning. Tom was taking no chances. He must have known he had guessed right . . . that they were above him with no way of reaching the launch except by using this trail. And he lay stretched out on his blanket directly in their path. Were his eyes open? They could not tell from where they were. When should they go? How much longer should they wait?

Pitch turned to Steve, his bloodshot eyes telling him to sleep, that it wasn't time yet. But Steve couldn't sleep. He could only watch and wait for Pitch's signal.

Finally it came. After looking at the luminous dial on his watch Pitch touched the boy's arm, then held a finger across his lips.

Now they were moving, their weight first on one knee, then on the other. On all fours they reached the trail. Quietly they stood up and took one step forward on the trail, then another, feeling carefully for loose stones and never taking their eyes off the giant figure below them.

Closer and closer. Don't breathe. Don't slip. Don't move a step until we're sure. He can't be more than ten feet below us. Careful now. His breathing is regular. His eyes are closed. Are we certain? It's so hard to tell, so hard. Is he sleeping? Is he waiting?

Another step, another lifetime. Pitch, oh Pitch, why are you stopping now? Go on. He's sleeping, Pitch. One step more and we're in the light. Another and another and we will have passed him. Oh, Pitch. Oh, Pitch. Go on.

A clawlike hand lay on the stone. Pitch's eyes were on it. Steve's, too, were drawn to it. The palm was turned up, all hard and calloused and lined in the yellow light. The fingers, curled at the ends, were moving . . . ever so slightly, it was true, but they were moving!

Tom was awake and waiting.

They pivoted as the hand reached for them. They ran back up the trail, their terror giving them the speed of wings. But they were wasting their energy, for Tom did not follow them. Only his laughter, insane and hysterical, pursued them. They heard it even when they were deep within the tunnels, safely away from him. Safe? Safe to be left to die of starvation within two weeks' time!

In agony they sat down on the floor of the tunnel, dreading the approach of the new day.

Dawn found them at the bend of the stream, staring into the gray light beyond the falls. They were not hungry although they hadn't eaten since the previous afternoon. With all hope of escape gone, they were conscious of nothing but fear. Their eyes were glassy and despair had claimed them completely.

Steve looked at Pitch, trying to find some solace in the fact that his friend's face was no longer swollen, his lips no longer black. It was funny, he reflected, that he should be giving even a thought to that now . . . when it didn't matter at all.

From outside they heard Flame's sharp whistle,

then the beat of his hoofs. And when all was still again Tom's shouts and cries came to them from the valley floor. But they couldn't make out his words.

They went to the great opening and crawled outside, ever fearful, ever careful.

Flame stood just below with only his nostrils moving; the rest of his body was rigid, and the cold light of dawn turned his coat into frozen fire. His eyes were on Tom, now scrambling up the trail.

"Tom tried to get up the valley," Steve said. "Flame stopped him. He stopped him just as I said he might, Pitch."

Tom reached the ledge. He stood there, his body rocking back and forth, back and forth. He put one hand up to his neck, his eyes. His fingers seemed to be digging, tearing into his very eyeballs.

"Oh, God, dear God, please help him," Pitch's lips moved in prayer. And Steve knew that neither Pitch nor he could bear any revenge toward Tom, only pity and sadness and fear.

Flame screamed again. And the sudden shrillness of it broke forever the slightest aspects of sanity which Tom had been fighting to retain. Now the mental fight was over. He screamed back at the stallion. He raced about the ledge, pawing the air with his hands, laughing, crying, shouting with no pause, going from one phase to the other, hysterically, madly.

It went on long after Flame had returned to his

band. Suddenly Tom looked up the trail and saw Pitch and Steve standing there, unmoving, their startled eyes fixed upon him. He became silent.

Pitch's hand found Steve's arm. But neither he nor the boy ran. They could only stare at Tom pityingly, helpless to do anything for him.

And he kept staring at them. Only when the colt neighed again did he finally turn away to look toward the canyon. For many minutes he watched the colt behind the gate, then focused his attention on the stallion and band that grazed a good mile away.

His gaze swept back to them. His lips moved without words. Then his voice came, deep and guttural. "Come down. I'll get your colt. I'll . . ." His lips continued moving but no further words could be heard.

They didn't have to hear the rest. They knew he was threatening to harm the colt if they didn't go down.

He stood there, rocking and waiting for a long while; then he turned away from them and watched the colt, the stallion and band again.

When Tom touched the whip about his waist, when he picked up two coils of rope from the ledge, Pitch and Steve knew he meant to carry out his threat. With fearful, terrified eyes they could only watch.

They saw Tom go to the valley floor; there he

dropped one rope at the foot of the trail and then went to the snubbing post and tied the end of the second rope about it. He walked swiftly and sure. His movements belied the madness that wracked his brain. It was as though he were now treading familiar ground and there was no fear within him. Yet his eyes never left the band and Flame.

They watched him walk softly, stealthily toward Bottle Canyon, toward the colt. Only Steve's eyes were alive. He didn't feel Pitch's arm on him. He didn't know he was being guided down the trail, a few steps at a time. He didn't know, although Pitch told him over and over again, that they were going to try to reach the valley floor while Tom went for the colt.

"We must wait until he reaches the canyon," Pitch said, coming to a stop just below the ledge. "He thinks he can get back before we have a chance of getting down the trail. But he can't, Steve. We can make it if we run hard once he's at the canyon."

The boy stood deathly still, his body rigid beneath Pitch's hand. Pitch wondered if Steve had heard him. Did he understand what they had to do? Pitch himself didn't dare take his eyes off Tom a minute. A few feet more and Tom would be at the canyon. Another minute and they could risk running down the trail. If they could only reach the valley without Tom's seeing them. If they could only get a good start, they'd have a chance, a real chance of getting away!

Pitch's body trembled. Tom was at the gate. The top bar came down, then the second bar. The colt moved out into the valley. Tom reached for his halter.

"Now, Steve!"

Pitch took another step down the trail, then froze in

his tracks. *Tom had turned around!* He was coming back. He was running his very fastest.

A sad whimper escaped Pitch's lips. For a few seconds he was incapable of doing anything but watching Tom racing toward them. Suddenly he came to his senses and started pushing Steve ahead of him. It was then that he heard the shrill, clarion call of the stallion, and he realized it was Flame who had caused

Tom to turn back. *If Flame had given them only a few minutes more!* Steve was going up the trail so slowly. Pitch pushed harder against him. He looked back at Tom.

But Tom wasn't coming up the trail. He had already passed it. He was going to the post. *He was going to fight Flame!*

Pitch turned to Steve. The boy had come to a stop, fully aware of the terrible, horrible drama about to take place beneath them.

Tom had reached the post. Arrogantly he stood before it, the coiled rope in his left hand, the bull whip in his right. "Come on, you stud horse! Come on!" he shouted at the top of his voice.

Flame swept across the valley.

17

The Fight

FLAME'S feet barely touched the ground as he came ever closer. His small ears were pricked forward and fire burned in his eyes. As he neared Tom, his ears swept back until they were flat against his head.

With the charging stallion less than a hundred yards away, Tom moved behind the post and cocked the wrist of his whip hand. He was ready.

Pitch said, "He'll stop him with the whip."

Steve shook his head. "He won't. He'll be killed, trampled."

They saw the long leather of the whip start to move when Flame was still fifty yards from the post. Tom brought back his arm. They couldn't see the leather as it streaked through the air, but they heard its pistol-like crack.

The sharp retort slowed the strides of the running stallion but didn't stop him. The whip spoke again, and now it cracked incessantly as Tom brought it back and forth, shattering the air. But Flame came on with dilated nostrils and thin lips drawn back. Screaming, he came to within fifty feet of Tom . . . thirty feet . . . and then he was within the range of the whip.

The leather bit deeply into his chest; he came to an abrupt stop, pawing furiously.

Steve closed his eyes. *Move, Flame. Move. Don't stand there!*

But the stallion only rose high in the air, seeking to pummel this long, snakelike thing that reached out to strike him. Again the whip bit into him, tearing at the softness of his belly. Screaming in rage and pain, he came down and the whip struck his chest. He rose, pawing, and once more the whip found his belly. When he came down, he stood still for a second, shaking in his fury, undecided what to do. His red eyes found the man who was standing a short distance away from him.

"Flame!" Steve shouted to his horse when he saw him standing still. "Go! Go! Go!"

Tom had been waiting for this precise second. Quickly he threw the rope and the noose arched cleanly in the air, then dropped over the stallion's head, settling around his neck.

Too late to avoid the lasso, Flame moved. He charged the man, screaming in all his fury and hatred.

Furiously the giant worked his whip, but the stallion came on, too close now to suffer the full impact of the long leather. Fear came to Tom's eyes as Flame sought his body with pawing hoofs. He kept the pole between them, narrowly avoiding the thrashing forelegs. He struck hard with the heavy butt end of the whip, which landed on the stallion's nose. Again and again he struck, always keeping the post between them, staying on his feet even when the pawing hoofs glanced off his shoulders. He was fighting for his life now, and this terrifying knowledge lent superhuman strength to the blows he delivered upon the stallion each time the horse reached for him with his raking teeth.

But there came the moment when Tom realized he couldn't keep the stallion away from him much longer. He kept moving around the post, kept hammering at the stallion's nose, and all the while his fear-crazed eyes never left those of the raging demon that rose before him. Soon one of those pawing forelegs would catch him hard and square, sending him to the ground. It would be the end.

Suddenly Flame came down close to the post, too close, for his shoulder brushed it, knocking him temporarily off balance. Tom moved quickly. Reaching down, he got hold of the rope that had encircled the stallion's hind legs. Pulling hard, he felt the legs give. The stallion tripped, then fell.

Turning quickly, Tom ran. He heard the pound-

ing hoofs behind him and knew the horse had regained his feet and was after him. But less than forty
feet away was safety, for the stallion was tied fast to
the post.

Steve watched Flame go after Tom, saw the rope
between the post and the running horse tighten,
then become taut, throwing Flame to the ground.

The horse was up almost immediately, fighting the rope that held him, screaming in rage.

A safe distance away Tom turned, frenzied hatred replacing the fear in his eyes. For a moment he just stood there, facing the horse, breathing heavily. Then he too screamed. He drew back the bull whip and then brought it forward, striking the tied horse who was pawing so futilely at it. Again the valley echoed to the terrible, horrible chant of the whip.

The red stallion plunged once, twice at the man who stood such a short distance away from him, who reached out at him with this *thing* that tore open his flesh. And each time he sought to reach him he felt the rope choking him around his neck. He plunged no more, now only rising to his full height to paw furiously.

As the beating continued, Flame ran around the post, the man following him, always reaching out with the whip.

"Fight me!" Tom shouted hysterically at the top of his voice. "You yellow-bellied stud horse!"

But the red stallion did not turn on him. He kept encircling the post, fleeing the whip. And as he did so the distance he was able to travel became shorter and shorter, the rope drawing him ever closer to the post and to a fate worse than that from which he now fled. But he had no way of knowing that.

Steve stood on the trail, watching the horrible

spectacle below. He was unable to move, unable to think. No part of him seemed to be functioning except his eyes, no part of him moved except his glassy eyes.

Pitch's arm was about his waist, holding him, but he felt nothing. Pitch said, "There's nothing we can do to help Flame, Steve . . . nothing." But Steve was deaf to all words, to anything but the rhythmic crack, crack, crack of the whip.

Smaller and smaller became the stallion's circle about the post. Suddenly, as though at last he realized what was happening, he stopped running away from the whip. Rising to his full height, he plunged away from the post. The rope held; the noose tightened about his neck, choking him. He went down hard and felt the *thing* tearing at his body. Scrambling to his feet, he plunged again, still seeking escape. He screamed as he went down; once more he felt the searing pain and pulled himself to his feet.

The stallion stood still, his body trembling. Tom snapped the bull whip to get him going again. A few more times around the post would be all that was necessary. The horse moved and he followed him. Twice more around and he had the stallion fast and close to the post. He picked up the second rope which he had left at the foot of the trail. Smiling, he made a noose, then lightly threw it on the ground. He waited until the horse stepped into it, then pulled the noose tight about the right hind leg. With nothing to fear now, he went forward and drew the end of the rope around the stallion's neck. He pulled hard and had Flame standing immobile on three legs. Then he tied the rope about his neck.

Next he grabbed one of the small ears. He twisted it savagely, bringing down the stallion's head.

"You can't stand having it twisted, can you? No horse can. You're not dealing with a kid now. I'm Tom Pitcher. I break your kind easy. I'm the . . ." On and on his lips moved. But at the same time he was using his hands. He had the rope unwound from the post. Now he brought the end of it toward the lowered head. He thrust it between the teeth that sought unsuccessfully to grab him, and bound the lower jaw; then quickly he brought the rope around the head and tightened it about the muzzle.

"A bridle you'll never forget . . . a war bridle, we call it. The pull is around your upper lip, your gums, too. You can't stand the pain, can you?" He pulled the rope once to make the horse aware of the additional pain he could exert; then he placed one arm across the stallion's back. A moment later he mounted, while Flame still stood on three trembling legs.

Pitch shook the boy but there was no response. He turned his own glazed eyes back to Tom. He saw

Tom's hand go to the rope about the stallion's neck which also held up Flame's right hind leg. He knew Tom was going to release Flame altogether now except for the vicious war bridle. He had seen all this happen many times before.

He saw the hind leg come down. Flame had the use of all four feet once more, but still he made no move. And the answer, Pitch thought bitterly, must be that Flame was beaten in body and spirit as completely as he and Steve had been. There was no reason for Flame or them to fight Tom any longer. Tom had won. Pitch closed his eyes; he didn't want to see the next sad phase in the life of this stallion who only a short while ago had been so noble, so proud, so . . .

Tom's yell, not in anger but in fear, caused Pitch to open his eyes. The stallion was rearing, and Tom was clinging to his neck. *Flame wasn't beaten!*

Tom dug his frantic, clawing fingers into the sweated coat. He was afraid to use the bridle rope lest he pull the stallion over backwards. He tried to get off, knowing that once he was on the ground he would have full control over the horse again. He drew up his long legs, ready to slip off the moment the horse began his forward descent. Then suddenly the small head came back; he knew then the stallion was intentionally going over backwards with him!

Unmindful of anything but to get free of the falling horse, he dropped the bridle rope and flung himself off the stallion's back.

He struck the ground hard and on the side of his head. He fought to retain consciousness. A heavy blackness descended, then a grayness. He tried to reach the light, which eluded him. And now he waited for the pounding hoofs to strike him. But nothing happened. When he was able to open his eyes, he saw the red stallion leaving him, moving along the end wall with the long bridle rope trailing behind.

Anger replaced the fear within him. Getting to his feet, he picked up the bull whip and followed. In body, if not in spirit, the horse was beaten and too spent to evade him for long. He broke into a run, his fingernails pressed deeply into the butt of the whip.

18

The Reckoning

PITCH'S arm tightened about the boy's waist. "Now, Steve. Now we can get away. He's forgotten us. He's . . ."

Steve was enveloped in a feeling of numbness, but Pitch got him to take one step, then another down the trail. He noticed that the boy's eyes were following Flame, following Tom.

"Flame's beaten, Steve. Do you understand? We can't help him. Move faster, Steve. Move faster."

More steps. Ever closer to the floor of the valley and escape. But Steve's gaze never left Flame and Tom.

The red stallion moved across the valley at a slow trot, so slow it was almost a walk. From about his small head trailed the rope of the war bridle. He made no effort to rid himself of it, perhaps because he sensed that it would be useless to do so. He stopped once and turned in the direction of the band far up the valley. But he didn't go to them, for Tom was between him and them.

Crouched low, the giant ran parallel with the stallion, keeping him close to the wall. An ugly smile played about Tom's lips. All he had to do was to keep the horse at this end of the valley, then close in on him. It was only a matter of minutes now.

He saw the injured colt just a short distance to his left. He cracked his whip, hoping to scare him away. He didn't want him around to get in the way, to spoil the fun. This fight was just between the stud horse and himself. It had begun that way. It would end that way. It wouldn't be long now.

The colt moved farther away, stumbling a little as he tried to go into a trot with his injured leg. But Tom paid no attention to him; his eyes were on the stallion and on the narrow canyon where the colt had been kept. His pace quickened as a new thought occurred to him. It would be more fun, more exciting if he could force the stallion down the canyon where he'd have him all to himself.

The whip cracked incessantly now in a large circular movement. Four beats, one to the right, one forward, one to the left and one behind. A rhythm, a chant, its tempo rising, becoming maddening. Going forward, the giant stomped and beat his feet to it as though he were dancing. His eyes gleamed, his lips moved but no sound came from them.

Seeking escape, the stallion turned into the canyon and Tom burst into a run as he followed him.

Pitch got Steve down the last few feet to the valley floor. Then he shook the boy in an attempt to rid him of his terrifying numbness. But he stopped when he looked into Steve's face. The boy's eyes were glazed and streaked with red. In them Pitch saw mirrored all the horror they had witnessed. And he wondered if his own eyes looked the same.

"Steve. Steve. Listen to me." He tried to keep his voice low and soft, but a shrillness crept into it. "We can go now. We can leave and get help!"

For a moment he was still again, just gazing into that smooth, lineless face before him . . . the face of a boy except for the eyes. They were sick, mature, even old.

"We're going now, Steve," he said, and this time he succeeded in keeping his voice soft. He pulled Steve gently, guiding him up the valley. A few feet, a few more feet. But the boy's head was turned back, back toward the canyon.

"We can't help Flame. We've got to think of the others now, Steve. We're leaving. We're going for help. Understand? We're going for help. We'll be back before he can touch the others." The boy turned to him, and Pitch spoke faster. "The colt. Think of him, Steve," he pleaded. "We'll be back in time to help him. But we must hurry now. We must get away. You must move faster, Steve."

Steve flicked a glance at the colt across the valley;

then the dullness in his eyes was pricked with pin-points of life, of understanding of what Pitch had said. His steps came faster, faster. *He was going to leave. He was going with Pitch to get help.*

Then came Flame's shrill scream from the canyon. Steve stopped, breathing heavily. He tried to deafen his ears to it, to listen only to Pitch's words urging him on. But it was no good, no good!

He twisted violently away from Pitch. He felt the man's grasping fingers on his skin, then the sound of his shirt tearing as Pitch sought a new hold on him. But he spun completely around. Now he was free and running! He turned to the end wall, to the canyon, *to Flame.* And he never heard Pitch's cries behind him.

He entered the neck of Bottle Canyon, his strides racing over the short cropped grass. The walls widened. Far down the canyon and to the right was Tom, his whip cracking. Steve didn't see Flame until he looked up the trail, and there he saw his horse climbing toward the cave and the crevice in the wall.

Not there. Not there, Flame!

Only to the ledge overlooking the spit of land did this trail lead; only to Lookout Ledge from where there was no escape, no turning back. It would all end there, the pain, the hatred, the brutality . . . for him and his horse.

When he reached the trail, Tom had followed

Flame within the cave. Steve's eyes were glazed with tears so he could hardly see. He stumbled, fell, and his nose crashed hard against the stone. He got up and, animal-like, used his hands as well as his feet in climbing.

He entered the grayness of the shallow cave, stumbled forward into the light from the crevice which split the rock above him. Just ahead was the ledge. A few more feet and he would see it all. But it was so quiet. No sound from Flame. No sound from the whip. No shrill words from Tom. Only silence. Was it over then?

He dropped to his hands and knees, then to his stomach, and pulled himself over the stone the last few feet. He looked out upon the ledge.

They were to the far left. He wasn't too late! Or was he? Flame was standing still except for the constant trembling of his gigantic body. His head was down, almost lifeless. From it stretched the bridle rope for twenty feet. At the end of it was Tom. He had the rope around the lower part of his great frame and all his ponderous weight was being used as he strained against it. The rope was taut and tight about the stallion's muzzle.

Tom had the bull whip in his right hand but he wasn't using it. Instead he was jerking the rope hard. Flame's head came up in pain with each pull but his rigid legs never moved.

Steve looked for a rock, for anything to use as a weapon against Tom. But there were no rocks on the bare ledge, nothing he could use. He'd go back to the trail. He'd find a rock there. He got to his knees, then suddenly fell down again, close to the stone.

Tom had straightened, had removed his weight from the rope, causing it to slacken. Flame's head came up in relief from the pressure about his mouth. All the pain he was suffering was in his eyes. But there was the glowing red of fire, too, fire that apparently meant more to Steve than to Tom. For Tom was going toward Flame as though he had nothing more to fear from the stallion.

Then Steve heard Tom begin to laugh. It came slowly at first and was nothing more than a chuckle. Then he was shrieking and screaming, his feet again stomping the stone in a frenzied dance. All the while he moved closer and closer to Flame. Behind him trailed the long leather of the bull whip.

Steve got to his knees. He knew Flame was going to bolt, to make another break for freedom. He would help him in any way he could.

It was then that he felt Pitch's arms closing around him from behind and pulling him backwards. He was being half-dragged. He fought hard and got his legs braced against the wall. The pulling stopped. He turned to face Pitch. He still heard Tom's laughter, but suddenly it was stilled beneath the scream of

the stallion. Clawing the stone, Steve pulled himself toward the cliff, dragging Pitch with him in his frenzy.

They saw Flame rising to his full height, while Tom backed away. He was still laughing but now it was more of a giggle. He kept backing, never taking his eyes off the stallion. Then he was crying, and his sobs wracked his tremendous body. Still retreating, he cowered before Flame, his whipless hand covering his eyes.

Pitch groaned, "Oh, Tom. Tom." He started to get to his feet, to go to him, to help him. But he was too late.

Tom kept going backwards, never feeling the dangling leather of the bull whip as it encircled his ankles. He realized nothing until he tripped and felt himself falling. Frantically he reached out to break his fall. But he was near the edge and there was nothing there but air. For more than three hundred feet to the spit below there was nothing to break his fall.

Steve saw it happen. He saw Pitch grab for Tom too late, then fall heavily on the stone. Pitch and the ledge began whirling crazily before Steve's eyes. And with it came blackness, spinning blackness. Steve slumped forward and lay still.

19

Conclusion

WHEN Steve regained consciousness, Pitch was standing beside him.

"Steve," the man said, kneeling down. The boy did not seem to hear him. "Steve," he repeated. The boy heard this time for his eyes focused on him. "He's dead," Pitch said. "Tom's dead. Do you understand? There was nothing we could have done. Perhaps it's for the best. Perhaps . . ."

Steve did not say anything. But he understood. He had seen Tom fall over the cliff. No one could have survived such a fall.

Pitch lifted the boy's head from the ground. "When you're up to it, we'll go back to the valley," he said. His voice was gentle; his words were simple and distinct as though he were speaking to a child.

Steve's head cleared when he sat up straight. He had fainted. But he felt no shame. He made a move toward the ledge, but Pitch's hands restrained him.

"Don't look over. It's better that you don't see him."

"But Flame? Where is he?"

"He's safe," Pitch said. "He went back . . . right after it happened. He's probably in the valley. We'll go there when you're ready."

Steve pulled himself to his feet. He stood still until he knew he was all right. Nodding to Pitch, he followed his friend through the crevice.

When they reached the trail, they saw Flame below them. Pitifully slow, the stallion moved up the canyon toward Blue Valley.

Leading the way, Steve quickened his pace; but he didn't break into a run until he reached the bottom of the trail. He spoke his horse's name over and over again in his mind, but the words never left his lips. Closer and closer he neared Flame. He saw the terrible lashes and clotted blood that covered his horse's body. He saw the long bridle rope trailing along the grass; even this seemed much too heavy for Flame to drag.

The red stallion's head came up when he heard the running footsteps behind him. Then he turned, his teeth bared once more.

Steve stopped. "Flame," he said. "Flame. Flame." His voice was scarcely audible. He went forward, repeating his horse's name over and over. Yards, then only a few feet separated them. His eyes were blurred. Flame was but a dark mass in front of him. He went forward, his hands outstretched until they found the wet and trembling body. He stood there, trembling too, and the tears that had welled in his eyes broke through and flowed down his cheeks.

When Flame had quieted down a bit, Steve glanced at the horse's head; it was lowered now. He moved toward it, taking the soft muzzle in his hands and loosening the rope from about it; then he pulled off the rope and let it fall to the ground without looking at it.

Steve took a step forward, and Flame moved beside him.

Only when they were in Blue Valley and nearing the pool did Pitch speak. "The first-aid kit is in my pack, Steve," he said. "There's gauze there and a bottle of antiseptic. Wash him clean and he'll get better. I'll leave him to you."

"Then you're going?"

"I'm bringing back the police constable this afternoon," Pitch said. "I want him to see where Tom fell. I don't want to move him."

"You'll go to the spit, not bring the police to Blue Valley?" Steve asked.

"Only to the spit," Pitch promised. "It happened there." Pausing, he added, "Tom's death was accidental, Steve. He fell. You and I know that to be the truth. That's what I'll tell the police. It's all they'll need to know. What Tom was like these past few days, what he did to us and to Flame is of no importance to them now. And Steve," Pitch paused again before going on, "Tom would never have gotten well. I know that."

They stopped when they reached the pool. Flame lowered his head still more to drink the cool, soothing water.

"It's over, Steve . . . *over*."

It was late in the afternoon of the same day when Pitch carefully brought the launch in toward the pier of Azul Island. Standing behind him were two men, both tall and thin and wearing white linen suits, black ties and pith sun helmets.

"Haven't been here in ten years," said one. "Just once, and that was enough for me. Why anybody would . . ." He left his sentence unfinished.

The other removed his hat and ran a handkerchief over his hairless dome. He said nothing, for he was watching the submerged rocks that seemingly grazed the prow of the launch as they approached the pier.

"Only Tom Pitcher would go and die in this God-forsaken spot," the first man spoke again. "As if we didn't have enough trouble with him on Antago. He was . . ." The man stopped, his eyes on Pitch's back. "I'm sorry, Phil," he apologized. "My sympathy."

Pitch said nothing. He had talked little since he

had picked up the chief constable and his assistant at the police station. He had answered their questions truthfully and he would continue to do so. But they hadn't been very surprised at Tom's death or the way he had died.

Pitch moored the launch to the pier. Then they walked across the wooden planking and stepped onto the sandy land. Climbing the dunes, they turned toward the mountainous yellow rock.

They walked in silence until the bald-headed man said, gazing up at the darkening sky above them, "We shouldn't spend much time here. No sense making all the trip back in the dark."

The chief nodded in agreement, then turned to Pitch. "All the way to the end of the canyon, Phil?"

"Yes," Pitch said. "At the foot of the cliff."

"You saw him fall?" the chief asked quickly. "I believe I asked you that before, Phil. But just for the record . . ."

"I saw him fall," Pitch answered. The constable didn't ask him from where he had seen Tom fall. He hadn't asked him earlier, nor did he now. He took it for granted that one couldn't have been anywhere else but below.

The yellow rock closed in on them, the end wall was just ahead. They saw Tom's body at its base. Pitch's footsteps lagged. The bald-headed man went forward while the chief constable stayed with Pitch, his arm going around him to lend support. "Easy now, Phil," he said.

The man had reached Tom. The body was heavy, but he was able to turn it over a little. He looked up at his chief and Pitch and nodded. Pitch turned away.

Later they all looked up at the precipitous wall. They saw the two protruding rocks and the rope hanging from them. Only Pitch knew that Tom must have thrown the ropes up when he had first reached Azul Island and had tried unsuccessfully to scale this wall.

The chief looked down at the foot of the wall again. He saw the pick. "Tom tried to reach the ledge, then," he said. It was not a question. He said it as a matter of fact, for it was so obvious that this was what Tom had attempted to do.

Pitch said, "Yes. He tried to reach the ledge." He was being truthful. Tom had tried and failed, and gone on to find another entrance to the interior of Azul Island.

"Why was he trying to get up there, Phil?"

Pitch spoke without hesitation. He had expected this question. He was ready for it. "Tom thought there was a habitable interior to this island," he said. "He expected to find out by reaching the ledge above." This, too, was the truth.

The man shook his head. "Just like him," he said.

"Always asking for it." He gazed up at the yellow rock, which gleamed in the sun's last rays. "Well, he got it this time. Everyone knows there's nothing there but rock, solid rock."

He hadn't asked if there was. He just said there wasn't. A statement of fact, requiring no answer.

"I guess that's all," the chief said. "I'll help carry the body, Phil. You get the pick, if you will." He was walking forward when he saw the bull whip lying on the ground a few feet away. "And there's his whip, Phil. Get that, too."

Pitch got the pick, then waited until the men had started off with Tom's lifeless body before he went over to get the bull whip. He reached down. To touch it was the most difficult thing of all.

"Phil! Let's get going." The chief had turned back to him. "It's late."

Pitch picked up the bull whip and followed them. Halfway to the pier he stopped to look back at the high wall; then, after a moment, he turned and continued toward the launch.

It was a month later and the valley was quiet again. The lower bar across the entrance to Bottle Canyon had been removed and now the colt dropped his head a little to get beneath the top bar. He went to the box of feed just within the canyon entrance.

Steve watched him as he played with the rolled

oats in the box, blowing through dilated nostrils, then, taking a mouthful, turned back to the gate. The cast and splint had been removed a week before, and there was no evidence of the fracture either in his appearance or movement. He had put on weight, too, during the last month and the size of his bones and recent development showed promise of his becoming a horse as large as Flame. He was broad between the eyes and jaws, his head well set on a strong, arched neck which entered the shoulders into good withers; his body was handsome yet rugged, his legs hard and flinty.

He would continue growing and getting stronger every day, for in addition to the rolled oats and grass, Steve gave him all the milk he would drink. His coat had a polished sheen from constant grooming. And never did a day go by that the colt didn't have his feet and legs handled and cleaned by Steve.

Now he ducked his head beneath the bar and came to Steve. The boy removed the halter, rubbed the colt's head where the straps had been, then put the halter back on. Snapping the lead shank to it, he led the colt across the valley, then back and around in a circle, again and again. He kept leading him until he saw Flame leave his band to join them. He unsnapped the lead shank then and waited for his horse.

The red stallion ignored the colt when he came to a stop before Steve. He stood still for a moment when Steve placed a hand on him, then he went to the barred entrance to the canyon. He snorted at sight of the oats in the box. But he couldn't get to them, for Steve wasn't giving him any grain. Flame's life in the valley was far different from what the colt's would be like away from the island. The great stallion lived only on grass as Nature had intended all horses to do. Flame's life was wild and free; he grazed where he wished in the valleys and canyons of Azul Island. But the colt would be leaving it all behind him within a few weeks. He would live for a while on a ship that would take him and Steve to the United States. Then they would be home. Not far from Steve's house were a barn and pasture where this colt would live and grow, with Steve watching him, caring for him.

Would it be as lovely, as good as this valley? No, in many ways it wouldn't. The colt would be giving up his life of freedom for domesticity. But in other ways it would be better. For he was a colt, soon to become a stallion. With Steve he was assured a long life, a life in which he could reproduce others perhaps like him. But here in Blue Valley he would be killed by Flame, just as colts before him had been killed. For Flame was a young leader and none would defeat him in battle for a long, long time. So it would be as Steve wanted it to be . . . the colt would go home with him.

Flame left the barred gate to move back to Steve, and the boy glanced for a fleeting moment at the scarred body where the whiplashes had healed. Then he turned away to look at the towering rock behind him. Somewhere in the tunnels Pitch was continuing his explorations, work that he had said would take him three to four years to finish. Three to four long years before he'd be ready to submit his manuscript to the historical society and let the world know what he and Steve had found here.

And so one might say, Steve thought, *that all our worries and fears are over. One might suppose that with Tom's death we could go on just as we did before he found us. Pitch has recovered all his relics and has found more. The snubbing post no longer stands by the pool. It's been taken down and burned. And no one on Antago is honestly sorry that Tom is dead, for he hurt too many people. The natives are again working the plantation, and they have nothing to fear any longer. So all in all one would be justified in thinking we could go on here as we did before.*

But it isn't quite that simple . . . not for me or Pitch or Flame. I've been in the tunnels only a few times since it all happened, and always with Pitch. It's never easy for me because I think I hear Tom somewhere ahead in the blackness. Silly; but that's the way it is. Usually Pitch takes me by the arm. I guess he does it to assure me everything is all right.

And it's the same with Flame whenever I ride him near the place where the snubbing post used to be or when we go through Bottle Canyon. He's restless, even a little afraid, although we've never again gone up the trail leading to the ledge overlooking the spit. I comfort him then because I understand.